Fishing with Dynamite

Fishing with Dynamite

B. Y. Randall

CB
CYANIC
BOOKS

For more information please contact:
info@cyanicbooks.com

First paperback edition October 2020

Book design by David Provolo
Photography by Phil Fernandez

ISBN 978-0-578-76092-6 (paperback)
ISBN 978-0-578-76093-3 (ebook)

Published by Cyanic Books LLC
Printed in the United States of America
No fish were harmed in the creation of this book.

For all the dreams we didn't chase…
but should have.

One

elcome to my life. Such as it is.

My name is Emma Connolly and I'm twenty-seven.

Sounds like some random support group opener, right? Relax. I don't suffer from any major disorders. Wait, that's not entirely true. Do sporadic bouts of terminal tedium count? People might think I'm an atypical millennial because I don't allow myself to be defined through a five-inch piece of glass or anything else with a backlight, meaning I don't tweet, follow, post, or like. All that stuff is methadone used to wean you off real life. Oh, and I don't do selfies either for one simple reason.

I know what I fucking look like. Jeez.

So, how exactly do I fit into the social briar patch? I'm not sure that I do, but then I've always been out of step.

It's allowed me to carry the weight of nobody's expectations but my own.

Growing up, kids hated me because I was one of those preternaturally gifted types for whom teachers always made exceptions. My talent was art. Put a pen, pencil, or paintbrush in my hand and it was pure nirvana for me. I was good, too.

Real. Good.

Being an only child, I used to sit in my bedroom for countless hours, just drawing and painting. I didn't go for the usual pursuits—playing with dolls, pretending I was a princess (I was, so why pretend?), or some other stereotypical bullshit they anchor you with when you're little. I didn't have a lot of friends, still don't, but I never really needed them.

I ruled in my own world of weird.

Two of my most formative memories both involved art, the first one when I was about eight. I was psyched to show my parents my newest creation; a watercolor painting of a pair of eyes crying multi-colored tears. No doubt it was inspired by the fact that I had heterochromia, something that I was self-conscious about as a kid, but as I got older I became proud of my mismatched eyes. They're not like Bowie extreme, but now I wear them as a badge of hipness.

Swelled with pride, I marched into the living room to unveil my latest effort.

Dad was glued to the Bulls game, while my mom was buried deep in some celebrity trash magazine. After being completely ignored for a minute, I promptly let out an ear-piercing scream of frustration and stomped out of the room.

Was I acting out? Probably, but my work demanded to be seen, even if I was seeking approval from a couple who bought decorative art at swap meets and only lasted twenty minutes at the Louvre.

That little episode earned me three months with a developmental therapist and an introduction to methylphenidate, but don't worry, I didn't suffer any lingering side effects from being dosed up so young. It actually fed my creativity by making me always look for the different in everything, so thanks, Mom and Dad!

The other influential event happened at age twelve when I started to hit the art contest circuit. I'd entered a local student competition for the suburban Chicago area and felt I had a pretty good chance for some kudos, but not any lame participation certificates.

I'm talking ribbons.

It came down to me and another girl who, honestly, had a way better painting. My boyfriend at the time was Rudy Packer, my much older man of fourteen who always smelled like Proactiv and puberty, and completely lacked anything remotely resembling social skills. When they surprised the living shit out of me by slapping that first-place blue ribbon on my frame, I pretty much lost it.

Rudy's reaction was somewhat different.

He was feverishly tethered to his Game Boy, and at my crowning moment of glory, he abruptly hurled the unit across the room in a fit of rage. Everyone just stared at him as he mumbled an apology. We broke up shortly after that, but it still underlined what had been a pattern in my early life.

A complete lack of support.

Sure, he was just a goof, but even a little positive reinforcement would've gone a long way back then. I've heard that Rudy went on to make *beaucoup* bank as a product manager for some big gaming manufacturer, while I struggled to pay the ComEd bill.

Oh irony, thy sting is vexing.

We lived in Portage Park, which was part of Chicago's Polish Patch neighborhoods, although our family was of Irish descent. This was never a big deal outside of the usual drinking jokes I occasionally got, almost all of which were awful.

Okay, one I liked. "An Irishman walks out of a bar. No, really."

My parents were lapsed Catholics, which fortunately let me off the hook. I'd always had a healthy mistrust of authority, so I could only imagine what life would've been like having to endure the usual church dogma. Christ, I got unruly at jury duty instructions.

We all floated in our own little universes, and the fact that we weren't exactly a tight-knit unit didn't really bother me. I was busy doing my art thing, Mom had her social circles, while Dad tried to recapture his high school athletic prowess in over-forty sports leagues.

Our tenuous strands also extended to my relatives, who were scattered across some nine states. I can't even remember a holiday where everyone came together in one big reunion, which was fine by me because I had some weird-ass fam. My uncle Vince was an ornithologist, and when he'd show up on that off-chance for Christmas, he'd always make me recite the state birds before giving me my present.

All fifty.

It remains forever drilled into my head. I'm not proud of it, and fuck you, scissor-tailed flycatcher, the one I always blanked on.

My Mimi, who was my mother's mother, was a real piece of work. Argumentative and petty beyond belief, she managed to get herself banned for life from all One Buck Only stores for abusive haggling. Now that takes talent.

I had another uncle who used to drop by unexpectedly, mostly to borrow money, and he'd always list in exhaustive detail everything that was physically wrong with him. I think the only things he ever left off his checklist were leprosy and bubonic plague, and this was almost always done over dinner. So tasty!

The list goes on and on, but I'll spare myself further humiliation.

Dad was a mail carrier and Mom worked retail, but when they were teens, they had their own creative outlets. She did ballet until about thirteen, then quit when she discovered boys, while he performed magic at birthday parties, until kids started to throw cake at him because he was so bad.

Logically, one would've assumed they'd be good at bolstering my confidence in my artistic endeavors. Isn't that part of the job description for all parents?

Riiight.

I got a lot of appeasing smiles from them, but never the full-throated endorsements I so desperately craved to let me know I was somehow on the right track. They were always more into The Big Picture.

My mom's philosophy about life that she tried to impress upon me was relatively straightforward, "Sit straight, shut up, and look pretty." She clung to vanity like Velcro, with a healthy dose of narcissism sprinkled in for flavoring, both traits I've resolutely resisted for the most part. Why go around telling everyone you're great? I mean, shouldn't they already know?

Realizing that my mom's viewpoint would do fuck all for me in life, I looked to my dad to dispense the deep think perspective on things. One time after lunch, it was just the two of us sitting at the kitchen table. He nursed a bottle of beer, then looked at me with that earnest expression parents have when they want to convey life lessons but aren't sure if their kid will get it.

"Honey, I want to tell you something important. Live the hell out of life now, because when you get to a certain age the world forgets about you. You understand?"

"Dad, I'm six," I replied.

He meant well, I suppose, and I'm sure eventually I'll find out whether it's true or not.

But damn, what if he *is* right?

I don't need to be remembered, but I do want to matter.

The one lasting gift I did get from my dad was his vocabulary, a treasure trove of profanity that has been embedded in me like some corrupt database. I make no apologies for it.

The bottom line is despite my fairly rudimentary upbringing, somewhere along the way I managed to carve out my own life philosophy. I'll try not to sound too pretentious about it, but here goes.

I believe everyone is born with a creative spark, some God-given talent, but out of either necessity or neglect, it eventually gets buried in most people as they grow up and move on with their lives. So that's my mission statement, plain and simple.

Okay, enough of my soapboxing, as I scream into the void.

Let's jump forward to my senior year, when everything changed. I was a student at Bellamy High, home of the Fighting Quakers. I'm not sure how many people got the absurdity in our school's team nickname, but I always found it amusing. Someone slipped one by and it just stuck. Right on.

The school itself was an old-fashioned Romanesque wonder, designed in the thirties with stone pillars, towers, and high arch windows. It literally was built like a brick castle that looked strong enough to withstand an attack from any Mongols or Cossacks, if they happened to be in the Chicago area.

My favorite perch was up in the bell tower, where I'd have lunch, draw, and wonder why nobody came up here on a regular basis to clean up all the bird shit that was lying around. It was so far beyond disgusting, but I still loved the place: the isolation of it, the compelling views it provided, and the fact that should a rogue tsunami hit the North

Shore, I'd be loving life. Location, location, location.

Senior Ditch Day was always one of the big social events of the year, and while everyone hit up Six Flags, the Cubs game, or assorted pool parties, I went to class. My rationale was how rebellious were you really being if you did what everyone else was doing? Lunchtime found me up in the tower again, sketching the main quad below, and it was there that I thought I heard the voice of God ask me a question that would forever change my life.

"Excuse me, who is your dentist?"

I looked around, confused by the seemingly disembodied inquiry. Not only that, but I felt guilty over having slacked off from regular flossing. Then again, how the fuck could they've known my oral hygiene routine? I finally realized it was coming from down below, and it wasn't the voice of God, it was Mr. Spangler, my seventh period art teacher. Flanking him on either side were two stern-faced faculty members, who looked at me with severe disapproval.

Mr. Spangler was in his early fifties, and the one teacher I had at school who encouraged us. He was tall with this shock of thick black hair, and he came armed with a wickedly dry sense of humor, which was one of the reasons I liked him so much. He was also the most popular teacher at Bellamy. I'd heard he'd given up a promising art career to teach our dumb asses, so I always felt sort of sorry for him. Not that teaching wasn't a noble profession and all, but I thought it should be what you settled for *after* you'd lived this rich and fulfilling life. Yet another in my endless stream of unsettling ideas about how the world should work.

Bewildered, I looked down at Mr. Spangler and replied, "Uh, Dr. Usrey. Why?"

"Because when you fall, as you most assuredly will, your dental records will be the only thing we'll have to identify you with. Just trying to save some time."

I looked down at the ground, looming some 100 feet below. "Maybe I'd just bounce," I countered.

"Interesting denial of basic physics, but how about we just let caution win out for now, shall we?"

"Okay," I conceded. I picked up my sketch pad and lunch and hopped off the ledge, doing a dance between the droppings on the floor.

My bestie at Bellamy was Natalie Farmer, a real misfit like me, but while I was always stupidly optimistic as a teenager, back then she had already descended into the deep end of the snark tank. She was adopted, which is probably where a lot of her anxiety came from, not to mention being a full-blown emo girl, always clad in the same basic uni consisting of a hoodie, Dashboard Confessional T-shirt, black Dickies, and Converse All-Stars.

She was self-consciously overweight, although at almost six feet tall, she carried it well. She had what she called "mood hair," meaning it would change color on a regular basis depending on her frame of mind. She even kept Manic Panic in her locker in case she wanted to modify herself during the day. I thought she looked best with the dusty mauve tresses, while she was partial to burgundy, tinged with aquamarine streaks.

Natalie was my touchstone, a yin to my yang, and never at a loss for providing an intriguing worldview.

"So, tell me again why I should give a shit?" Natalie asked as we trudged down the hall of the main admin building lugging our JanSports and our drama. "You have yet to convince me."

"Because it's graduation!" I offered, knowing it would do nothing to sway her opinion.

"Exactly, which means I'll probably just sit there and cry the whole time. Remember me at the end of that fucking dog movie?"

"What dog movie?"

"The one with Jennifer Aniston. Remember how I couldn't even talk for an hour afterwards? Graduation is going to be like that, but on roids."

"What for?"

"Because once we chuck those stupid little hats in the air, that's it. I'll never see any of my friends again, and I don't have that many to begin with."

I don't want to say Nat was a drama queen, but I did buy her a rhinestone tiara for her sweet 16.

"You'll go to college and make a whole new set of them. What's the big deal?"

"Em, I've got a 2.8 GPA. That's an express pass to some reject juco. Let's face it, I'm going to be thrown out into the real world, and just the thought of that is scary as fuck to me."

"C'mon, how can you not be excited about the future?" I happily declared.

Jesus, I made most beauty pageant contestants sound like sullen bitches.

"You're right. That cashier job at my dad's paint store is looking *sooo* inspiring."

"Natalie, there's a million things you can do."

"Spoken by 'The Girl Most Likely to Succeed.'"

"Oh please."

"Please what? Look at you. I'm not the one who's stylish, talented and hot."

"I'm not hot," I shot back.

A side note on this. I'm average. I'm five foot five, have diar-
rhea-brown hair, and I'm whiter than Vermont with a smattering of
freckles. If that's not textbook average, I don't know what is. I will
confess to being somewhat of a clotheshorse, however, always keenly
aware of fashion, even with my limited funds.

As we got to the end of the hallway, Natalie wasn't through, not
even close, as she projected the next twenty years of my life.

"You'll get some scholarship, become fabulously successful, marry
some delicious man candy, and squirt out a brood of ungodly beautiful
children. It's all been predetermined, Em."

"Okay, you're nuts. Listen, I gotta go. Call me later."

I trotted on ahead as Natalie yelled after me. I think she'd sponta-
neously combust if she didn't always get the last word.

"I'm holding you responsible if I wind up leading a life of envy
and self-loathing."

While I carried a 3.9 at school, all my other classes paled in comparison
to my art class. It was there that I came alive. The rest was rote institutional
crap. I knew I was going to be an artist for a living, so could we please just
dispense with the earth science, calculus, and world history? I know those
courses were to help make me a well-rounded individual, I get it, but in
the ten years since I've left high school, never once has the sovereignty
of Chechnya taken center stage in my life.

The art class was held in a drafty old room that was always freezing.
Made my nipples look like corn silos. I swear the place doubled as a
morgue after we'd leave, it was that uncomfortable. My station was in
the back, chosen for the cover it provided when sneaking late-afternoon
snacks and far from the main line of sight.

On this particular day, I was working on an acrylic painting of animals morphing into cars. One could say it was Daliesque, but I never really fashioned anything I did after anyone. It was just based on my own unique perspective of the world, fed by an abnormal imagination. Or maybe it came from the fact that I was ambidextrous, which supposedly meant I had a higher creativity level. It also meant I probably had the gene that was linked to schizophrenia. There's something to look forward to.

People were always telling me that my art was very accomplished for someone my age, although I always took that as somewhat patronizing.

Good was good, no matter what age.

Mr. Spangler was walking through the room, checking out everyone's work, when he stopped by my station and whispered to me.

"Please see me after class."

Normally those words will instantly freeze any student's blood, but he said it with a faint smile, so I was hoping it wasn't all bad.

Strolling back to his desk, he came up with one of his patented quips we all loved.

"Now people, lest you forget, your final projects are due on the 20th. And that is using the modern Gregorian calendar and not some wonderful invention of your own."

As class cleared out, I packed up my shit and walked to the front desk, where Mr. Spangler sat reading a magazine.

"Hi, Mr. Spangler, you wanted to see me?"

"Yes, I did."

And he offered nothing more, as a few awkward moments filled the air. He just continued reading.

"Uh, okay..." I sputtered.

There were a few more quiet beats, then I officially started to get spooked. I sensed something bad was about to be dropped on my pointy little head.

"Am I in trouble or something?"

This got Mr. Spangler to put down the magazine and look at me.

"Assumption of guilt. Never offer it because it immediately puts you in a position of weakness."

He got up from his desk and walked to the window that overlooked the front of the school.

"Come here, Miss Connolly, and tell me what you see."

I joined him by the window and saw a group of students hanging around in front of Bellamy, the school day over.

"A bunch of kids. Why?"

"Anything else?"

I had no idea what he was getting at. "Is this supposed to be like a moving Rorschach test?"

He laughed and shook his head. "No. Now, when I look out, I see a sea of potential. Of course, the majority will probably lead unremarkable lives, distinction eluding nearly all."

"Kinda harsh, but okay."

"Oh, I don't say it to be mean, and I love teaching kids, but it's just reality. Yet there are exceptions when you just know someone is possibly meant for greatness. Yourself, perhaps?"

He turned and looked at me, then reached inside his jacket and handed me an envelope.

"I didn't want to send the Arts Institute an email because it will never replace the resonance of a formal letter. It's what us old farts do."

My eyes went wide. My heart raced.

"Thank you, thank you for doing this!"

"How could I not? You browbeat me into submission."

"I'm sorry. I just really wanted this."

"No need to apologize. You deserve it. And just so you know, in twenty-four years of teaching here I've only had a few students that have had the raw talent you do. I give you this on one condition, however, and it is a tough one."

Shit! And I was thisclose to freedom.

"Which is?" I wondered.

"You go out and amaze the world."

Please, at least *try* and give me something difficult.

Mr. Spangler walked back to his desk. "And in response to your earlier question, yes, you are in trouble. The vice-principal was less than enamored with your choice of lunch venue, but I was able to negotiate him down to two days of detention on your behalf."

Even this bit of bad, but not entirely unexpected, news couldn't piss on my parade. You've got to understand why this was important to me. After all those years of having little or no creative support system, here was someone who finally believed in me. He had written a recommendation to try and help me get into the Chicago Arts Institute, which I positively knew I would get into.

And guess what? I did. A full fucking scholarship.

Sometimes things were predetermined, just like Natalie said.

Two

T he first two years at the AI were pretty unremarkable, even by my undemanding standards. I took the requisite courses in art history and the humanities, as well as the usual smorgasbord of liberal art electives. Meanwhile, the actual painting courses were heavy on theory and conceptualism.

Zzzzzz.

Sure, it's good to have roots, to know the basics of how to do what you're doing. Now let me throw some names at you.

Frida Kahlo, Basquiat, Van Gogh, Grandma Moses, and Rousseau, the painter, not the philosopher. By the way, did you know he was the one who coined the phrase "Let them eat cake," and not Marie Antoinette? Look it up. The slut just stole it.

None of them ever had proper training, they just painted. Although I knew I'd never achieve one scintilla of what any of them accomplished, I'd always felt a kindred spirit, and if I ever ran into them in the afterlife, I'd high-five them all.

Socially, life was exceedingly bland as well. I hung out with a lot of awkward creative oddities who constantly listened to nothing but dinosaur music like Bauhaus and Rush. I even had a roomie who used to masturbate to photos of Robert Smith when she thought I was asleep.

Speaking of sex, I had three serious boyfriends when I was there, two of whom I wound up devirginizing. Defiler of youth, that was me. They were all nice, but it was nothing more than filling each other's loneliness gaps until it was time to move on.

And I discovered the liberating powers of weed.

I had tried it a couple of times in high school, but it was so prevalent at the Arts Institute you could get a contact high just walking between classes. Of course, the faculty discouraged it, reminding everyone that recreational use was *verboten* and we were all going to wind up in Cook County lockup if we kept doing it.

For me, though, it unshackled my lizard brain and lit up my artistic impulses like the Northern Lights, which I'd actually seen while I was there. Something called a coronal mass ejection had occurred, which made the aurora borealis visible as far south as Chicago, so a bunch of us piled into an SUV and drove up the lakefront to see it.

We laid out on blankets tripping on shrooms and eating Nutella with our fingers out of the jar, while Dead Can Dance blasted from the SUV. The combination of the shrooms and the lights blew my fucking mind like nothing ever has before or since.

I recommend it highly. Literally.

Anyway, this is all context and background leading up to the big epiphany I experienced in my third year that set me on the course I wound up taking, for better or worse.

Definitely worse.

There was a weekend bender at a friend's off-campus apartment, a sordid bacchanal with too much beer, not enough food, and some of the dankest-ass kush I'd ever smoked. It was about two in the morning and I was sitting on the couch holding an empty bong, wondering when the pizza guy was going to show up. His tip was growing smaller with every passing minute.

The room was strewn with passed-out bodies, enough discarded red Solo cups that Christo could've made an exhibition out of it, and the stench of spilled fluids, bodily and otherwise. This was major carnage. The CDC wouldn't have ventured near here even in hazmat suits.

Back to my epiphany. I always thought if I had one, it would come to me in a dream or a Native American sweat lodge. That would've been epic, but no, it arrived in a cloud in my brain, and way before the pizza did.

After the haze parted, and in a cleansing moment of clarity, I remember thinking, that's it. It's over.

I had no idea of what the actual fuck I was going to do with a BFA in Studio Art. I was hardly teacher material, and let's be real, the world wasn't waiting with open arms for another starving artist, and I liked eating. I didn't have much money growing up and sure as hell didn't want to continue that inglorious tradition. Suddenly, it didn't matter how good I thought I was, or what people told me. In that very moment, the thread to my life had become totally unraveled.

So with a year and a half left toward my degree, I dropped out.

Was it impulsive? Foolish? Self-sabotaging? Possibly. Only time would tell, and so far it ain't said shit.

There were other factors that played into my decision as well, things that just kept building and building until it all finally gave way.

Like one giant human sinkhole.

I had a minor health scare, as I developed a cyst on my back that just got bigger and bigger until I thought I was going to have to name it. I was already planning what dress I wanted to be buried in, an uber-cute Moschino LBD I had bought for Christmas.

What better way to show it off than with an open casket?

When I finally went to see the doctor, I promptly embarrassed myself by wrecking the Visible Man display in the examining room. Like some adolescent troublemaker, I touched the midsection and the whole stomach lining fell on the floor right as the doctor walked in. There I was, on my knees gathering up plastic intestines in front of the man who would pronounce my fate.

It turned out to be an epidermoid cyst that had formed, most likely from my poor loofah habits. It was excised, and a great burden was lifted off my shoulders, although anything like that does give one pause to think.

There was also trouble at home during that time. My dad had just run off with a woman named Debbie Beswick, who was the captain of his bowling league team. To be fair, she did carry a 186 average, which obviously proved to be catnip he couldn't resist.

So just like that, twenty-two years of marriage went up in smoke, although truthfully, it was pretty much a wisp from a fire that'd gone out about fifteen years earlier. This devastated my mom, and I eventually moved back in with her. There were long, painful nights where she would bemoan what had happened to her, and I, the dutiful daughter, tried to cheer her up. After about four months of cauterizing herself from the world, Mom discovered the wild, wild west of online dating, met a new man, sold the house, and moved away to Decatur with him, all in short order. She seemed happy, while my dad got dumped by Debbie, but then found new love with a female pitcher on his recreational softball team.

God, he was such a sports whore.

After all that upheaval, I found myself alone and adrift. I decided to move back to the city, where I bounced through a series of jerk-off jobs until I finally wound up selling toner cartridges for a company called STC. If you're dying to know, it stood for Superior Toner Cartridge. Any guesses how many rocket scientists it took to come up with that moniker? The business was part of some multi-tentacled conglomerate that also spewed out office supplies and pressed wood furniture, which I heard somewhere could be toxic.

Death by desk. Sweet.

I really didn't care about the company all that much, although I'd always secretly wished we'd have a turf war with one of the big-box retailers because I swung a mean-as-fuck desktop hole punch.

I once tracked my lineage, only to find I hailed from a long line of commoners.

Secretaries, mechanics, people involved in the custodial arts, and now here I was joining that stellar lineup with what I was doing for a living. My fate was inexorably sealed.

At least I had a window cubicle so when my mind wandered, which was 95 percent of the time, I could sit and stare out at the world, musing on the folly of my existence. That's not to mention also having a ringside seat for some great wrecks at the corners of East Washington and North State.

If you haven't been able to tell by now, I've got a gallows sense of humor blacker than the ink they used to fill up the crummy cartridges I tried to sell. I suppose it's a defense mechanism, something I came up with to keep from getting torched on a pyre of crippling self-doubt.

How's that for rationalization?

I worked in an office full of fellow underachievers. Couldn't tell you half their names, as I pretty much kept to myself, content to punch the clock and collect a check. The only person I was tight with at work was Tami Hamaya, a Japanese alpha female who genuinely liked her job, which annoyed me to no end. It's not like we hung out a lot, but at times she was seemingly the only one who kept me from taking a header out the window when the monotony became too suffocating.

So now you're all caught up. Feel free to judge. I know I would.

"Can I speak to the office manager, please? Yes, my name's Emma Connolly and I'm calling from STC. Oh, hi. Can I ask you something? Are you currently happy with the toner cartridges you're using? Well, STC does offer very competitive prices on the best cartridges on the market. Would you like to have a...?"

The phone went dead in my hand, a reaction that had become so routine, I was stunned when conversations lasted longer than a minute. They had trained us into believing that cold calling was not just a numbers game, but also an art. After two years of doing it I'd come up with a very simple response to that school of thought.

Go fuck yourself.

It was a depressing, demeaning, and demented (triple word score for awesome alliteration!) way to make a living. So why did I do it? Because I wanted to have a roof over my head, gas in my car, and money for my weed dealer. Could I have been doing something else to make a living that wasn't so soul-crushing? Absolutely.

Why wasn't I?

Because I was a chickenshit who had become a well-worn tread on the path of least resistance. And it was with this humiliating introspection that I picked up the phone to wade back into the trenches.

"Good morning, may I speak to the office manager? Emma Connolly from STC. I'm calling about toner cartridges. Well, I don't think that's anatomically possible, but thanks for the suggestion."

I hung up and stared at the pictures pinned to my cubicle wall. Ah, the happier times. Cancun, Paris, Montreal. None of which I'd ever been to, but if you're going to create a facade, make it count.

I had been to the Grand Canyon and Vegas once, but tacking up photos of that would've made me look like some trailer park trash. I had an image to project, er, protect.

"C'mon, Em, time to go to the principal's office."

It was Tami, my aforementioned co-worker, who you'd actually smell before you'd see her, as she always wore the most delicious Chanel perfumes. She was tiny, yet possessed by this enormous energy that bordered on ADHD. She was a life force I secretly envied.

It was me ten years ago.

"No," I firmly declined.

"No? Ooh, Em, I like that. Rebellion."

"What's the point? They're just going to tell us what a shitty job we're doing."

"Well, what a shitty job *some* of us are doing," she said as she sat down next to me and flashed that megawatt smile of hers.

"Jesus, Tami. You look like the kid who just found their dad's favorite jizz sites."

She giggled with excitement. "I just landed Symetron. Got them to commit for all of their Midwest offices."

Tami sniffed the air and looked at me with a curious expression.

"Do you smell that?"

"Smell what?"

"Promotion."

"Yeah, you're practically drunk with power."

I looked around the office where all the other salespeople were fighting the good fight, giving their phone pitches while their souls ebbed away. Conformity to the nth degree.

"Tami, do you ever look around here and say, 'This can't be my life'?"

"No."

"Figures. God, how can you be so amped at ten o'clock in the morning?"

"Because I've got three Red Bulls and half a pack of Camels in me already. Breakfast of champions."

Our monthly sales meeting was always held in a conference room with an annoying electrical hum that sounded like a swarm of angry bees had gotten stuck in a turbine. The district manager, a corporate droid named Elliott Dornan, stood in front of a whiteboard going over pie charts. I called him Human Tryptophan because he always put everybody to sleep.

And as usual, he was being a dick.

"The numbers for the third quarter were off 13 percent. Now I'm not one to point fingers, but it does start with you people in sales," he droned on.

With that bit of good tidings, he was cancelled.

Tami nudged me and slid her tablet over. It had a full-page ad for some beastly SUV on it. Attached was a sticky note that read, "I take delivery Friday. Fine AF."

I scribbled down, "Congrats. Pay me back the hundred you owe me." Tami saw my response, and a blank look suddenly crossed her face.

Meanwhile, Elliott added to his *bonhomie*, "In short, the stockholders aren't happy. And if they're not happy, I'm not happy. And if I'm not happy...well...I'm going to make your lives miserable."

With our monthly pep talk over, Tami and I walked back down the hall to the cattle crates.

"Nothing like boosting company morale by threatening you."

"C'mon, Emma, don't take it personally."

"How else am I supposed to take it?"

"You're right. You suck," Tami summed up nicely. "So, where do you want to go for lunch today?"

"Can't. I'm meeting Aaron."

"Why are you still seeing that guy?"

"Why wouldn't I be?"

"Because he's a loser."

I stopped walking and slapped her on the arm. "What is wrong with you? You say that about everyone I date."

"Possible trend developing here."

Elliott walked down the hall and motioned to Tami.

"Tami, can I see you for a minute?"

"Sure."

Tami gave me an excited look, then turned and followed Elliott down the hall. She glanced back and pumped her fist.

Jee's Spot was a funky Chinese restaurant in the theater district that I loved for their name and killer har gow. The lighting and service were lousy, but it was a fair trade for how great the food was and the fact that you didn't have to crack open a 401(k) to pay for it. Aaron and I would often eat there after a game or show and usually wind up closing the place down.

We'd been dating for a couple of years and it was comfortable. I was a pretty low-maintenance girlfriend to begin with, and although he lived and breathed sports 24/7, we somehow made it work. I might as well tell you now. I'm not a big sports fan. Never have been, never will be. I know that's practically heresy in a place like Chicago. Maybe it's just a subconscious rebellion against my dad. I was happy when the Cubs finally won the World Series, but that was mostly because it was like a national holiday to get fucked up and act like an idiot for a few days along with everyone else.

I originally met Aaron at Lollapalooza when I unceremoniously passed out while waiting to use the port-a-crapper. It was hot as balls and I had quite the choice. Wait in the mile-long line for water because I was completely dehydrated, or the equally ginormous line for the toilet. I chose not to have major organs rupture on me. When I came to, Aaron was next to me offering a beer to bring me back to life. Not exactly textbook CPR, but in a pinch it did the trick. He was my knight in sweaty Under Armour, and soon after, we started seeing each other. He was like a choir boy gone bad, with his angelic face, golden curls, and impish personality.

Aaron worked as a bartender at an upscale hotel near Millennium Park and, unlike me, made it through four years of college, getting his Bachelor's in history from Loyola. He had no earthly idea what he was going to do with that, though, as I think it was mostly for his parents. Oh, the sacrifices we make as children.

As we chowed down on our appetizers, Aaron stared at me across the table with that sly grin of his.

"What?" I smiled back.

"Em, do you have any idea how special you are to me?"

"Aww, baby, I feel the same about you."

"The way you laugh, the way you smile. The way you make me bust with that thing you do with your thumb."

Great. Nothing said romance more than discussing my astonishing sexual technique over a plate of steamed dumplings. I blushed Hellboy red as he continued.

"No, I'm serious. I think about that all the time. And believe me, you have no idea how much I'm going to miss those things."

"Why?"

"Long version? Because this just isn't working out for me."

When I was a kid, I once put a knife in a toaster to try and remove a piece of stuck bread. I accidentally touched a coil and was knocked back about four feet.

That feeling had returned.

"Jesus, what's the short version?" I managed to stammer out.

Just then, our waiter came over with our orders and rudely set them down in front of us. I glanced at my plate, then up at the waiter.

"Excuse me, what's this?"

"Yu-Shiang pork with spicy fragrant sauce."

"But I ordered the moo goo gai pan."

"No, you didn't."

"Yes, I did."

The waiter took his order pad out and showed me what he had jotted down.

"That's written in Chinese," I protested.

The waiter huffed and walked away, leaving me to deal with the situation at hand. Food I didn't want, and a boyfriend who no longer wanted me.

"Doesn't this look absolutely delish?" Aaron said as he sized up our meals, twirling his fork in ravenous anticipation.

By this time I was so shook, a brain wave scan of me would've probably looked like a 7.9 on a seismograph.

"What do you mean it's not working out? Aaron, I don't understand. I thought we were happy. In the two years we've been together, we've never even had a fight."

"I know and I think that's part of the problem."

"That's a problem?"

"Yes. I was reading that couples that don't fight actually have very fucked up relationships. They just don't know it. Bee-zarre, huh?"

He knew that it annoyed the shit out of me when he affected words like that, so this was clearly a case of him spiking the ball in my face. What a fucking troll.

Aaron aimed his fork at my plate.

"May I?"

He didn't wait for an answer, as he stabbed a forkful and wolfed it down.

At this point numbness had begun to set in as I tried to mount a defense, pitiful as it was.

"I can't believe you're saying this."

"Don't worry, baby, it's not your fault. I'm just restless. I guess I'm evolving and you're not."

"'Evolving'?"

"Yes, I'm not the same person I was two years ago. You are."

"And that's bad?"

"Not bad, just...inhibiting."

I leaned back, trying to articulate the thousand questions that ricocheted around my mind.

"I don't get...how long...are you seeing someone else?"

"Oh honey, no, please don't think that," Aaron pleaded.

After a moment he responded, "But yes."

It was times like these that reminded me, it's not how you fell, it's how you got back up. No thanks, I thought to myself, I'll just sit here and play in my pile of emotional shrapnel.

I cut out of work early citing a medical problem, and I'll be fucked if having your heart ripped out doesn't qualify. I crawled back to my apartment, a small place in Bridgeport on the South Side that was bereft of much personality, but it was affordable and relatively safe. Some people gave me worried looks whenever I told them I was a Southsider, but that was their problem. Bridgeport had been listed as one of the four most ethnically diverse neighborhoods in Chicago, and it was also home to the world-famous breaded-steak sandwich, neither one of which saved me a dime on rent.

Back to my crisis, I wasn't really mad yet at having been dumped. I was still too shell-shocked for that. In fact, it was almost like an out-of-body experience, as if I witnessed it happen to someone else.

I fell on my couch and replayed the whole lunch episode in my mind, yet foolishly hoped there was an alternate ending. A colossal waste of time if there ever was one.

The truth was I felt emptier than the men's room at a BTS concert.

I knew what came next.

The purge was about to commence.

Time to remove all traces of Aaron from my apartment. Clothes, tchotchkes, anything he might've left behind.

There was one small problem. There wasn't anything.

I tore through the place, looking for tangible proof that someone had once shared my life. The closest thing I found was a ticket stub for a Blue Man Group show we went to, but then I remembered that I paid for that.

How the fuck could there not have been a single shred of evidence? Then it struck me. He must've been planning his escape for some time, slowly extricating himself from the whole relationship. I begrudgingly admired his stealth and had half a mind to call him to suggest a new career in crime. Total ninja.

Aha! I finally found one remnant of our time together. Stuck in the corner of my bedroom was a stuffed Pikachu knockoff that I'd won at a pop-up carnival. You know the type, where evil workers enslave customers and disappear in the middle of the night, never to be heard from again. For some reason, I'd developed a strange attachment to it. Maybe it was the deranged smile glued to its face, which had started to peel off. Ultimately, I knew if I wanted to make a clean break, it had to go.

I grabbed the fuzzy, lumpy, yellow blob and marched out to the living room, shoving it in the nearest trash bag I could find.

There. The slate had been wiped clean.

That lasted for about a minute, as I walked right back and rescued it from the garbage heap. You don't throw away a Pokémon in any incarnation, and if you did, you were just asking for ten years of bad juju. I had a huge collection of stuffed animals as a little girl, and when my mom gave them away without telling me, I was absolutely gutted.

There were certain things that just transcended the world of sexual politics, so I tossed it in my living room closet. Out of sight, out of mind, but never out of heart.

I sat down on the couch and flipped through the mail when my cell phone rang.

"Hello?" I answered.

On the other end were the sounds of pneumatic drilling and other assorted industrial mayhem. I heard a male voice yelling at someone.

"Tell him to put a tourniquet on it. Are you joking? Because he's squirting blood all over the garage. That's why!"

"Hello?" I said louder.

Finally, after the noise died down, a voice came on the other end.

"Hi, can I speak to Emma?"

"This is her."

"This is Brad from Crown Motors. Listen, we went over your car. It looks like you've got a cracked head gasket."

"Swell," I groaned. My beloved Mini Cooper was hurting. I'd had it for about seven years and took better care of it than I did myself.

"It'll be about $2000 to repair. I can send you over a detailed estimate. What do you want us to do?"

I would've sold a kidney to fix it. "Like I have a choice? Go ahead and do it. I just hope the credit card company doesn't send hitmen."

"Should be done by next Wednesday. We'll call you when it's ready."

"Thanks. I'm sure it'll be the highlight of my day."

I hung up, took off my shoes, and threw them across the room. I was never really one for neatness, and now that no one was coming over to share my humble abode, what did it matter?

The doorbell rang and I walked over to answer it.

Standing there to greet me was Claudia, my grizzled old landlady, who was a biker chick back in the seventies. Both her arms were completely tatted up, and she spoke in this rasp of a voice soaked in nicotine and Jack. She used to regale me with stories about her torrid love affairs with various members of the Leather Angels of Hell motorcycle club in Skokie, and suddenly a thought occurred to me.

Who better to ask about what to do over my current relationship debacle?

JK. Her advice probably would've involved bone saws and body parts.

Today wasn't a social visit, however, as she simply held up my returned rent check with a big red "NSF" stamped across it.

I looked at the check in disbelief.

"Take care of it," Claudia growled as she turned on her heel and walked away.

I closed the door, still staring at the check. How could I have been overdrawn? Look, I never would've made it as a forensic accountant, but for Christ's sake, what pinhead couldn't balance a checkbook?

Apparently me.

I plopped back down on the couch and just started to laugh. How many people in one day get kicked to the curb, told they need $2K to fix their car, and then find out they bounced their rent check? Most people would spread that out over a few months or so, but here it was all neatly wrapped in one giant clusterfuck.

I finally opened my laptop to check my email. Maybe some Nigerian prince was offering to save me or, better yet, I'd find some enticing offers for penis enlargement.

What I found was an email from the alumni association of Bellamy High. It was an invitation to my ten-year class reunion themed "Hello/Goodbye", and boxes marked "Yes" or "No" awaited my input.

Three

Here's wisdom. Beneath my veneer of cynicism beat the heart of a sentimental slob. I don't mean I got all damp when I saw pictures of puppies or babies or dopey Christmas movies. That shit was lame. And for some reason, I didn't miss people as a general rule. No, I wasn't some misanthrope, I just had trained myself to be self-reliant, or maybe it'd been hardwired since youth. I don't know, but here's the strange thing.

I missed places.

When I would visit somewhere I hadn't been in a long time, it gave me a rush of nostalgia that was hard to describe. It made for this strange mashup of happy and sad, as I immediately tried to sort out the good times from the bad generally associated with the place. Like a few years ago when I went to visit our old house that my mom had sold. It'd been a while since I'd last seen it, and I made mental notes of all the changes. The color of the house was different, my favorite Norway maple tree was gone, and the front lawn was dead from neglect. I had half a mind to go pound on the door, bitch slap the owner around, and tell them to get with the program. This was the house I grew up in. The only one I had ever known. My immediate arrest would've probably followed, however, so I sulked from across the street.

It was with mixed emotions then that I stood and stared at the main admin building of Bellamy High, the institution that had claimed four years of my life. Fortunately, the good outweighed the bad, but then when I figured in how far I hadn't come in ten years, the needle immediately dipped back into the negative. This is where a lot of dreams were born, not just for me but for everyone who'd passed through those stone portals, and now it was about to be razed. Something about asbestos, or earthquake codes, or some other bullshit excuse so someone could rape the land and make buttloads of cash.

I was ambivalent about coming to the reunion in the first place, mainly because I'd always heard that only two types of people attended these things. One was "The Success," looking to gloat over all the people who'd dissed them as teens, and the other was "The Stunted," those whose lives had peaked in high school and were looking for a way to crawl back into yesterday.

I was neither, more drawn by the fact they were going to tear down my school and I wanted to see it one last time. A banner reading "Thanks For 70 Wonderful Years" hung from the front of the building, which was beautifully bathed in blue and orange lights, Bellamy's colors.

People brushed by me as they headed to the reunion, while I just stood there and stared at the edifice. I picked out windows that I had sat next to in class, gazing outside, wondering how and when life would start for me.

"Isn't it fucked up what they're doing to this place?" said a girl that I noticed out of the corner of my eye.

"Totally. You can't tear it down. It should be declared a landmark."

"What do you say we kneecap the pricks responsible?"

I shot her an uneasy sideways glance, then it took me about five seconds for it to completely register. I couldn't believe it.

"Natalie!!" I shrieked.

I gave her a fierce hug, then took a step back to take in what was a much different Natalie. It was shocking. Gone was the anxiety-ridden girl I knew ten years ago, and in her place was a confident-looking, professional young woman. She had this gorgeous blunt cut, light years from the uneven multi-colored mess she'd always had, and she was wearing a form-fitting designer dress. We're talking real *haute couture* here.

"Wait a minute, who are you again?"

"Version 2.0, baby."

"I mean, your hair, your clothes. Everything. You look amazing. What happened?"

"I literally woke up one day and realized how absolutely pathetic I was. Still this fat, bitter emo girl with no future, so I dropped thirty pounds and decided to join the human race. I'm lucky they let me compete. You don't look too shabby yourself."

"It's all smoke and mirrors."

"Yeah, right. Okay, Em, so we've got a decade to catch up on."

I threw my head back and moaned, "God, don't say that. It makes me feel so old."

"You are old, girl. You're twenty-seven. If you were a rock star you'd be dead."

Natalie yanked me by the hand to follow the crowd. "C'mon, let's go. I want you to thrill me with your tales of adventure and eroticism."

We got our nametags and just to fuck with everyone, we switched them. The embarrassing thing was no one seemed to notice. Or care. A photographer was roaming around and coaxed Natalie and me into the requisite stupid shots together where I probably looked like the poster child for a hostage video. We straggled over to the main auditorium and listened to our senior class president bore everyone to tears with his welcome speech. I then proceeded to lose half my net worth trying to win some craptastic raffle prizes.

The main reception took place in the gym, where we stood with drinks in hand and tried not to mingle. The place had been decked out with blowup photos of students and events from our graduating class. Jason Mraz songs blasted over the speakers. I was already pretty buzzed, as Natalie surveyed the crowd and pointed out various partygoers.

"Hated that girl, liked that guy, have no idea who that is. Ooh, always wanted to fuck him."

"Still holding back," I teased.

"Always. I'm starving. Let's get something to eat."

We walked over to the food table, where Natalie loaded up on carrot sticks and celery. I stared at her in disbelief.

"What?" she asked defensively.

"Four years and I never saw you eat a single vegetable."

"Yep, I've gone total vegan. It's awesome."

"I'd probably become homicidal if I ever gave up red meat," I said, picking up a slider.

"See, that's what I thought, but after a month of detoxifying I felt like another human. God, I was shitting out battery acid for a week."

"And that takes care of that," I shuddered, totally put off by her vivid description. I set the slider back on the tray.

"Fill me in. What've you been doing? Where are you living?"

"I'm still in the city. What about you?"

"I moved down to South Beach."

"Nuh-uh," I said as I stared at her, stunned.

"Yep. Started a furniture business and it blew up massively. My husband and I now have three stores in Miami and we're making *sick* money."

I peered at Natalie intently.

"No, seriously. What have you done with Natalie?"

"I know, sellout, right? Believe me, for someone who grew up with basically nothing, I feel so guilty sometimes. I give a lot to charity."

"And you got married. Any kids?"

"Three. One of each."

I tilted my head, warily intrigued. "I'm afraid to ask what that means."

"Boy, girl, and adopted."

"I'm officially jealous."

Natalie snapped a bite out of a carrot and nodded.

"Uh-huh. Now tell me about your charmed life. Go ahead, make me feel like garbage."

I looked at my drink, then around the gym. I was stalling because I didn't want to lie, not to my best friend from high school, and I felt ashamed to tell her the truth. Especially after she had gone and turned into the Martha Stewart of South Beach.

I nodded toward the exit door. "Let's go outside. This music is killing me."

We walked out to the main quad, where some couples had retreated, including a pair who were dry humping on a table.

Natalie nodded toward the couple. "Nice to see some things haven't changed."

"I used to eat at that table," I said.

"So, you still live in the city and what else? I keep expecting to see you pop up on your own reality show or something like that."

"What in the world are you talking about?"

"Hell, I don't know. Oh wait, hang on! There's this brand-new thing called the interweb. You should check it out. It's a great way to stay in touch and stalk your frenemies."

I shook my head. "Yeah, I don't do anti-social media. I think anything you post can and will be used against you in a court of law someday. Tell you the truth, I'm not even sure why I came here."

Natalie's cell phone suddenly went off. She fished it out of her jacket, looked at the screen, and grunted.

"Fuck, I gotta take this. It's one of my suppliers in Bangkok."

"Sounds vaguely criminal."

"Do not go anywhere. Okay?"

"Promise," I said, holding my fingers up in the Girl Scout sign.

Natalie grinned, then walked away speaking Thai on the phone. Thai?? Natalie used to wrestle English to a draw.

I wobbled over to a table to finish my drink, which I downed in a straight shot. I crumpled the cup and took aim at the large trash can nearby. With deadly accuracy I fired, missing by six feet or more.

Thoroughly embarrassed, I looked around to see if anyone had seen my pathetic display of athleticism. Thankfully, no one had. I lurched back to my feet to dispose of the cup properly.

Once again upright, I began to wander around the courtyard recalling all the countless lunches and bullshit sessions I had had here. I looked up at the bell tower, my old familiar haunt, which still loomed over the complex. My first thought was how incredibly dumb I was to have sat on the ledge up there, but when you're a kid, you're fearless. This was immediately followed by me wondering if someone had finally cleaned up that shitsty in the last ten years. Wishful thinking, no doubt.

I walked over to the main building with a total balloon on me and in need of immediate relief. I stepped into the hallway, where a janitor was making his rounds.

"Can I help you?" he asked.

"Don't tell me. I'm trying to remember. Restroom is down that way?"

I gestured to the left, totally confident in my sense of recall. He pointed the opposite direction.

"I knew that," I bluffed.

"Hurry, we're going to be locking up."

"Sure thing. Just as long as it takes me to puke my guts out."

The janitor gave me a look that said I'd better be fucking joking.

"Just kidding. Kinda. Sorta," I assured him.

Situation resolved, I came out of the bathroom and wandered down a quiet hallway. I stared up at the ornate ceiling as the memories washed over me. The place even smelled the same. Feeling frisky, I took off my shoes, my nylon-clad feet rubbing against the cold, slick floor. I thought, what the shit, I'll never get this chance again.

I put down my shoes and measured out a decent parcel of land. I took off running, then broke into a standing slide as I glided across the marble floor. I was quite pleased with myself considering I'd never survive stepping out of my car for a drunk stop the way I was.

I walked back to get my shoes, and as I slipped them on, I noticed a figure at the far end of the hallway. I peered closer.

No way, I thought.

"Mr. Spangler," I said out loud to myself.

He disappeared around a corner, and I walked down the hallway after him. I wanted to say hi, but as I came out to where I thought he'd be, Mr. Spangler was nowhere in sight.

Figuring he'd probably gone back to the old art classroom, I sluggishly climbed the stairs. I reached the landing and caught my drunken breath, then walked over to the room and looked inside. All was quiet.

As I continued to stare, I thought, this is where it all started once upon a time.

I was about to head back downstairs, but I quickly grabbed the railing for support. The alcohol had rapidly tapered off my motor skills, and a rest was most definitely in order.

Like now.

I sat down on the top step, leaned against the wall, and closed my eyes, letting my mental bumper cars have at it.

"Miss Connolly, have you been drinking?"

I woke up with a start, trying to get my bearings and let my brain reboot. "What? No," I answered to no one in particular.

I glanced around and realized it was a question that came from Mr. Spangler, who was standing behind me with a smile on his face.

"Wow, Mr. Spangler. Hi."

"Hello, Miss Connolly. It's good to see you."

"You still teaching? Wait. Of course you are. Why else would you be here? Stupid-ass question."

"I'm still here."

I staggered to my feet, holding on to the railing for dear life.

"I recommend you stay seated until the ride comes to a complete stop," he advised.

"Great idea," I concurred, and sat my butt down again.

"How's the party going?"

"Interesting, I guess. Everyone is pretty much the same. Well, almost everyone. My best friend, Natalie, has turned into a titan of industry, which I never would've figured, but I'm thrilled for her. It must be those twenty-year reunions where people start to morph into aliens, huh?"

"Something like that," Mr. Spangler laughed.

I looked up at him, trying not to sound like an inebriated fool, then proceeded to do just that. "Do you know I think you were my very, very, *very* favorite teacher?"

"That's a fairly weighted title to live up to, but thank you. And as I recall, you were one of my best and most talented students."

"Really?" I asked, with more than a tinge of desperation.

"Absolutely."

"Cool. Thanks," I said, momentarily marinating in the praise.

"What have you been up to?"

I started to answer, then stopped. That was it. I couldn't pretend anymore, so I did what anyone who's been hiding for years would do.

I burst into tears.

"Why does everyone keep asking me that?" I agonized.

We sat on the hallway steps together, my eyes swollen from crying, as I worked a tissue into oblivion. Thankfully, Mr. Spangler spoke in that supportive, non-judgmental tone of voice that had made all the students love him. It was something I really needed about now.

"What made you drop out?"

"Fucking *life*," I blurted out as I worriedly looked at him. "Please don't be mad at me."

"Why would I mad at you?"

"Because you wrote that incredible letter to help get me in."

"Yes, but your ability as an artist is what actually got you in."

I ran that thought around for a few laps, then shrugged in agreement. "Okay, it's a tie."

"And now?"

"And now I'm a worker bee."

"Do you still paint?"

I shook my head. "I sometimes doodle at work. Does that count?"

This was not going well. Facing yourself never is.

Suddenly, the lights went dark. Closing time, and they'd forgotten all about me.

"Terrific. Now I'm going to be locked in," I grumbled.

"Don't worry," he said. "We'll find a way out."

Mr. Spangler and I spoke a little longer, then said our goodbyes. I came back out into the main quad, where the reunion crowd had started to call it a night. I noticed Natalie talking to a balding, heavyset guy in his late twenties. He casually stroked her arm as he spoke, but she was clearly not into it.

Upon seeing my return, Natalie shot me a look like she wanted to strangle me for abandoning her. She tried to pry herself away from the conversation.

"Listen, I have to go," said Natalie to the stroker.

"C'mon, at least call me," he protested.

"No, Jeff, I'm married."

"So am I."

"Well, great. Have your wife get in touch with my husband then. We'll have a fourway."

"Really?" he asked excitedly.

"Fuck no!" Natalie hissed. She yanked her arm away and came over to me. "You're a horrible Girl Scout. Where did you go? I almost had to break out the Mace."

"I'm sorry, I had to go to the bathroom. Who is that guy?"

"Jeff Ordway."

"Like in first boyfriend Jeff?"

"The same."

As we walked away, Natalie looked back at him. He held up two fingers in the "call me" sign.

"No! And I want my virginity back!" Natalie yelled.

We followed the departing crowd, but Natalie was still revved and ready to roar.

"Okay, this thing was a total buzzkill. What do you want to do now?" she declared.

"Food. Lots of bad food," I said firmly.

Romano's was a family-owned pizzeria near Bellamy that had been the student haunt for over forty years. With their patchy red checkerboard tablecloths and faded mob movie stills on the wall, it was tacky as hell but still home. Natalie plowed through a plate of asparagus risotto, while I gorged on the greasiest, most Keto-unfriendly pizza I could've humanly ordered. Nearly empty bottles of red and white sat between us, further contributing to the dance party that was occupying my skull.

"God, I was hoping to run into someone that I actually liked, but..." said Natalie.

"Gee, thanks," I cut in.

"You didn't let me fucking finish. When I saw you, I realized that

I didn't give a shit who else was going to be there, number one on my wish list was present and accounted for and that's all that mattered."

Jesus, Natalie had me about three seconds from going full-on booger cry.

"Nat, are you trying to make me go all hormonal?"

Joe, the owner, who looked like an enforcer for a crime syndicate, stopped by to check on us.

"You ladies doing okay?"

"We're fine, thanks," I smiled. "Do you remember us?"

Joe leaned back to get a better take, looked at me, and nodded.

"I remember you."

He turned his attention to Natalie, struggling to place the face. She saved him the trouble.

"Forget it. Existing technology wouldn't help you identify me."

He returned his focus to me. "But yeah, I do remember you."

He walked over to the table next to us and lifted the tablecloth.

"Oh my God," I gulped as I dropped my head, totally mortified.

Underneath the tablecloth, on the table itself, was a drawing I had done years ago with a black felt-tip pen of a giant bowl of pasta with strands hanging out that were legs.

"You did this," said Joe.

I shamefully nodded. "Does this mean you're going to spit in our dessert?"

He laughed and shook his head.

"You think I would've kept it all these years if I was mad? I thought it was great."

I was so relieved. It's not often you can get away with defacing someone's business property and still get complimented on it.

Natalie nudged my hand. "Autograph it for him."

"Stop," I scolded her.

Natalie picked up one of the bottles. "Can we get another Sangiovese, please?"

"Coming right up," said Joe as he walked back to the bar.

"Hey, you're never going to believe who I ran into tonight. Remember Mr. Spangler?" I said.

"The art teacher? Wore tweed coats and smelled like musk?"

"Yep."

"I always thought he was kind of hot, in an old guy sort of way."

"That's him."

Natalie laughed, as I looked at her, puzzled.

"What?" I said.

Natalie pulled the wine bottles away from me. "I'm cutting you off."

"Why?"

"Because you're *non compos mentis.*"

"I don't know what that means. I took two years of French, not Latin."

"Means you're drunk as fuck, Emma."

"Tell me something I don't know."

"Uh, okay. How about Spangler died two years after we graduated?"

I've never been slapped, but I felt like someone just did it.

Hard.

"Get out of here," I meekly protested.

"Yep. Had a heart attack and dropped dead right after seventh period."

My mind was reeling, trying to process the impossible.

"There's no way. How do you know?"

"Because if you're a geek at heart like me you still keep up with alumni news."

She pulled out her phone. "Albert Spangler, Bellamy High, Chicago," she voice-searched. Natalie held the phone up for me to see a group of stories, all with the same common thread mentioning his passing.

I just sat there numb, staring at a picture of Mr. Spangler on the screen.

"No, you don't understand. It was him. I...I...had too much to drink is what I had," I tried to reason, while my face probably resembled chalk by now.

Natalie put her phone back and pulled out a business card and handed it to me.

"Before I forget, here's my email and number. Swear you'll keep in touch?"

I nodded, but honestly, the rest of the evening was pretty much clouded by utter confusion. I know what I saw, and simply put, I'd never felt more freaked the fuck out in my life.

Four

I once read that in the early sixties in Chicago, there was a place called the Garrick Theater that was torn down. It was a gorgeous old palace, and despite a huge public outcry, it still wound up on the business end of wrecking balls. There was a well-known preservationist named Richard Nickel that tried to save it who said, "Great architecture has only two natural enemies: water and stupid men." A brilliant fucking comment, if there ever was one.

I flashed on that opinion while I sat in my car and watched as the cranes plowed mercilessly into Bellamy. Why was I even here? A few other people were hanging around to document the destruction on their phones, but I guess I was just there out of respect. That and the fact I had a bit of a melancholic streak in me that I liked to indulge in every once in a while. It cleansed the palate.

I got out of my car to take a closer look and walked to the construction fence that had been erected around the site. They were up to where the administrative offices had been, so it was no great loss yet, but I knew once they started knocking down the classrooms and bell tower, I'd totally lose my shit.

As I watched, I caught a glimpse of something in one of the

classroom windows. Was I seeing things again? Nope. Well, yes.

It was Mr. Spangler staring out at the demolition. He looked over, saw me, and waved.

Instinct kicked in as I immediately scurried to one of the construction foremen to try and get his attention.

"Hey! Hey, you guys...there's someone...you gotta stop."

The foreman finally noticed me, came over, and took out his earplugs.

"Can I help you?"

"Yeah, there's a..."

I looked back up, and the window I had seen Mr. Spangler standing by was now empty.

"Is there something wrong?" the foreman asked.

The wrecking ball smashed into another part of the building with a loud crash. What was I really going to say to this guy anyway? Ghosts had squatter's rights?

"Yeah. You guys suck," I said and stomped off.

I think it was a Tuesday that my world slipped off its axis. It's strange that I don't quite recall exactly when it was, because I'm usually pretty good with dates. Birthdays, anniversaries, when my cable was due to be disconnected because I was always late with the bill.

The alarm had just gone off and I was still in that nebulous zone, the one where five-more-minutes was locked in a steel cage death match with get-your-ass-out-of-bed. That day the latter won, so I rolled out of the rack and walked bleary-eyed into the kitchen to fumble my way toward breakfast. I poured a big bowl of cereal and walked into the living room, eating and dropping Cinnamon Toast Crunch along the way. In case I needed to find my way back, the path was clearly marked.

"Did you take these? They're really very good."

"Thanks," I said reflexively.

Wait. What?

Through gunk-crusted eyes, I looked over and saw the compliment had come from Mr. Spangler, who was perusing some framed photos I'd taken that were hanging on the wall.

I gently put the cereal bowl down on the counter and, without further interaction, walked back to the bedroom, closed the door, and let out a bloodcurdling scream.

I locked the door and leaned against it, trying not to hyperventilate.

I had no idea what was happening, but on the insanity chart, having the ghost of your high school art teacher show up in your apartment had to at least merit top-ten status. That thought was immediately followed by me being mad at myself for having such a fucking messy place, even if the guest was unannounced. Maybe my mom was right, vanity does trump all.

I stayed in the bedroom for another couple of minutes, trying to formulate some rationale for what I had just seen. Finally, I decided to face my fears and grabbed a nearby golf club.

Cracking the door open ever so slightly, I peeked out. There was nothing there. Slowly, I opened the door and proceeded down the hallway, club firmly in hand. As I reached the living room, I thought my heart was about to burst from my body, I was that frightened.

I warily looked around the empty living room.

"Do you golf?"

I whirled around. Mr. Spangler was now standing in the kitchen.

"What?" I said breathlessly, then looked at the club I was holding. "Oh. No. This is my dad's."

"That looks like a vintage mashie niblick. They're worth quite a bit of money."

"Great, I'll put it up for auction."

"Are you all right?"

I let out a disbelieving laugh. "Are you joking? You're asking me? What are you doing here?"

"I'm here to help you."

"Do what? End up in a psych ward?"

He walked out of the kitchen as I backed up against a table, knocking over a flower vase.

"You seem a bit agitated, Miss Connolly."

"Gee, I don't know, maybe it's because I'm talking to a dead guy."

"Oh, I'm sorry, I thought you knew. Don't you stay up on alumni news?"

"You and Natalie should get together," I mumbled to myself.

"Well, yes. I'm a 'dead guy,' as you so inartfully put it, but it's all right. I've made peace with it."

"No, you haven't," I protested.

"Excuse me?"

"You wouldn't be here if you did. Ghosts are people who haven't reconciled their past and can't move on. I watch Discovery Channel."

All right, Em, smack that shit down!

Mr. Spangler laughed. "Complete random psychobabble. Tell me, have any of those 'experts' who spout such idiocy ever interviewed us to get our side?"

I could see it now. I was going to be late for work because I had to stop and engage in a debate about metaphysics. I had to put a pin in this.

"Okay, Mr. Spangler, I don't know how to put this, but my life is in total free fall right now so the last thing I need is a ghost…"

"Spirit," he corrected me.

"What?"

"I prefer spirit. Ghost is such an unexceptional term."

Far be it from me to ever back down on an argument involving semantics, but I relented.

"Whichever. Doesn't matter. Either way, I don't believe in them."

"Well, I believe in you. And I still believe in your talent."

"What talent?" I sneered.

"You're an artist."

"No, I sell toner cartridges. That's what I do."

"A mere detour."

"Please, just go before I become completely unhinged," I pleaded.

"Go where? I have nowhere else. The school was torn down."

Holy shit, I just got dealt the sympathy card from the bottom of the fucking deck. Well played, Mr. Spangler, well played.

I relaxed my grip on the club as I maneuvered my way around the living room. A thought then struck me, and I grasped the club tighter.

"How did you even find me? What is there, some kind of ghost GPS?"

"The spirit world affords us many possibilities."

"Okay, that's creepily cryptic. I've gotta go to work. Just please be gone when I get back. I can't even."

I had made my way back to the hallway, where I turned and bolted back to the bedroom.

I don't remember driving to work that day, that's how tweaked I was from the early-morning encounter. I just knew that when I got there, I wouldn't be able to focus on anything. Well, that was essentially the case most of the time, but especially so on this day.

I didn't know who to talk to about this without sounding like a major headcase. I figured Tami was the logical choice. She was the one I was closest with at work and might be an empathetic ear.

I found her in the break room, surveying the snack vending machine.

"Tami, we need to talk," I said in a hushed, almost conspiratorial tone.

"Do you realize there's not a single healthy item in here? A diabetic could sue the living shit out of us."

"Great legal insight. Seriously, I have to talk to you."

"First, you have to congratulate me."

"On what?"

Tami held her arms outstretched. "You are looking at a newly minted regional sales manager. Meet your new boss."

"Congrats."

"Got a raise and my own office too," she boasted.

"You bust that glass ceiling."

"And my first job is to get all you lackeys into shape."

"Good luck with that," I snorted.

I decided to close the door for extra protection, just in case someone walked by and heard me detailing my problem. That's how whisper campaigns start.

I pulled Tami over to a table and we sat down.

"What's up? You look all jumpy," she said.

"I need you to keep this between us. Swear?"

"C'mon, Em, we're tight."

I nodded, then tried to think of the ideal way to broach the subject. Figuring the direct approach always worked best, I looked Tami in the eye and lowered my voice.

"Do you believe in ghosts?"

She laughed. "Hell no. Why?"

"Because I've seen one and now it's in my apartment."

Tami stared at me with a concerned look.

"Getting dumped has really fucked you up, hasn't it?"

I slapped the table in frustration, trying not to lose my temper.

"Don't you think I know how whacked this sounds?"

"Obviously not, or you wouldn't have mentioned it. Look, Em, if that's the problem, I know someone you can talk to."

"Really? Like a spiritualist?" I asked hopefully.

"No, I was thinking more along the lines of a really good therapist."

"Okay, we're having two different conversations."

Tami suddenly perked up, her eyes flickering with excitement. She grabbed my hand. "I've got it, I've got it. Em, listen, I'm going to do you a huge favor, and you're going to love me for it, but you can't tell anybody."

I gave her a guarded look. "What?"

"I'm close with HR now."

"So?"

"I'm going to go down there and talk to them for you."

Anyone have a clue where she was going with this? Because I sure didn't.

"I don't get...what are you talking about?"

Tami leaned close to me. "I'm going to ask about you getting two mental health days off. And *nobody* gets two days around here. Unless, of course, you're management or straight-up 5150."

"I gotta go," I said with a disgusted sigh.

"You'll thank me."

I got up and left the room. I looked back briefly to see Tami wiggling two fingers in a reconfirmation of her offer.

I came home from work completely exhausted as usual and with one immediate plan. Get out of my work clothes and get on the console. I tossed my keys on the kitchen counter, then froze.

I remembered I might not be alone.

"Hello?" I asked suspiciously.

I walked into the living room and did a quick survey of the area. Nothing. There was no life, passed on or otherwise.

I stuck my head inside the bedroom and glanced around. Empty.

Things were looking good. Perhaps my plea had been heeded after all.

Content in my solitude, I took up my favorite position on the couch armed with all the creature comforts anyone ever needs: food, drink, some chronic, and my controller.

My one concession to the ruling zeitgeist was that I was a gamer. I loved my electronic opioids, mainly *Horizon Zero Dawn*, the greatest game ever made. I played to relieve stress but, more importantly, to save the world on a daily basis, albeit a post-apocalyptic one. Gaming gave me a sense of accomplishment I didn't get IRL. Sounds good, right? Jesus, Freud would've had a fucking field day with us.

I did play by myself, however, because there were just too many freaks and neckbeards to contend with out there in the multiplayer world.

I periodically looked around just to make sure I was still alone and then I was off to do battle.

"Is this really how you're going to spend your evening?"

I hopped off the couch and spun around. Mr. Spangler was sitting in a chair behind me.

"Yes," I stated with blunt conviction.

"You do realize video games are truly insidious, don't you? They're thoroughly counterproductive and sap you of your will."

"I love my time sucks, now leave me alone. I'm about to level up."

"Miss Connolly, you used to be so optimistic, it was practically infectious."

"Yeah, well things change."

"Evidently not for the better."

He nodded toward the big Bob Marley King Size spliff I was holding. "Is that for medicinal purposes?"

"Yes. I'm hoping enough psychotropics will make you disappear. Apparently, I need a stronger strain."

"Have you tried Laughing Buddha?"

"What? Yes. It makes me dizzy."

"Durban Poison?"

"That gives me panic attacks."

"Nine-Pound Hammer?"

What the fuck was going on? I was being quizzed about my weed preferences? How did he even know this shit?

"Mr. Spangler, what do you want from me?"

"To see you succeed. Do you know why you're not happy?"

"Stab in the dark here, but let's go with because I'm probably on the verge of a nervous breakdown?"

"No. It's because you have no creative interests."

"I just spent nine hours at a dehumanizing job. Do you really think I can come home and be creative?"

"Why not?"

"Try it sometime. Well, not now, but..."

A thought immediately went through my mind. Is there political correctness regarding ghosts? Hmm, I wondered. And as long as we were getting things out in the open, I felt compelled to get this off my chest.

"Do you realize what you guys never taught us?"

"Enlighten me."

"What to do when all these great plans we make when we're young turn to total shit."

There, I had just asked The Great American Question that so many before me never had.

You're welcome.

"Yes, because if we did, we'd be sending out a fleet of depressives," he explained.

"Okay, you're probably right. How dare you defeat me with logic."

Mr. Spangler walked to the dining room table, picked up a magazine, and pointed to an ad.

"Here. 'Draw Sniffy and win $10,000.' My God, you could do this in your sleep."

"That magazine is like twenty years old. I think Sniffy has already been drawn and probably quartered."

He put the magazine down and picked up a brochure from The Creative Complex, one of those adult education companies which offered tons of courses that no one ever admitted to taking.

"What about this then? They have lots of interesting classes. Photography, sculpting, all kinds of things. It's the perfect way to express your artistic needs."

"The only need I have is to be left alone."

"So, this is really going to be your life?"

I raised my hand. "I vote affirmative."

"I have an assignment for you."

My arms flew up in total frustration. "Oh my God, you're kidding, right? This has gone so far beyond the teacher-student dynamic."

"I want you to think about when it was that you gave up on your dream. Not the exact day, mind you, but approximately when you said to yourself, 'That's it, world. Count me out. I quit,' and then please get back to me."

Mr. Spangler walked to the living room closet, stepped inside, and closed the door behind him. I just sat there staring at the closet in stupefied silence. I finally got up and walked over to the door, hesitating a moment before I opened it.

Three questions spun around my brain. What the hell was he doing in there? What if my walk-in had somehow become a portal to the afterlife? What if it was a total shambles?

I yanked it open, and my worst fear had been confirmed. The closet was a complete disaster. Mr. Spangler must've thought I was some horrible hoarder with the way it looked. Stop me if you've heard this before, but I'd been meaning to take all this stuff down to Goodwill, but just hadn't had the time.

Regardless, he was nowhere to be found.

If Mr. Spangler was insistent on staying, or at least popping up from time to time, I had to lay down some ground rules. I taped a sign to the wall leading down the hallway stating simply: "You DO NOT come anywhere past this point." I realized there was no way to actually enforce it, but I was relying on him being a gentleman to respect the privacy and sanctity of my bedroom. Not that there was any action going on in there anymore, but more in case I wanted a quick session with B.O.B, a girl's best friend in time of need.

And Christ, did I need it now.

Back at work, I sat at my desk and looked over The Creative Complex brochure. Okay, so maybe a small seedling had been sown, but as I leafed through it nothing caught my eye. Tami walked by and clapped her hands.

"C'mon, Em, let's get some calls going. I get pressure, you get pressure."

"Yep, it's a vicious cycle," I said as I held up the brochure. "Do you know anybody who's taken one of these courses?"

Tami snatched the brochure out of my hand and laughed at it.

"Oh my God, this thing is still around? No way. These classes are strictly for losers and guys who can't get laid. Don't tell me you're thinking of signing up for one?"

"Not really."

"Listen, management asked me to ask you because we're friends. They want you to ditch the nose stud. They're on this whole company image makeover and they're starting with you guys."

"You have to be kidding me."

I couldn't believe they were taking umbrage with this small gold nose stud I had gotten when I turned twenty-five. It was to commemorate the milestone, and I guess my own small symbol of trying to maintain some degree of edginess before I slipped into my decrepitude.

"I've always got your back, Em, but there's only so much I can do," said Tami, trying to put her best good cop face forward.

"Yeah, yeah."

What the fuck was next, I had to start coming to work dressed like Offred to cover my two tiny tattoos?

Five

T he Siffredi Gallery was a low-rent place in River North, nestled in between all the other tonier galleries. It was used primarily for experimental photo exhibits and wrap parties, but I was there because it was also moonlighting for a drawing class.

Yes, I signed up in a moment of weakness. I accept your scorn and derision.

A group of people milled about in the outside lobby armed with sketch pads and pencil kits. I hung out off to the side, chomping on my gum as I took in the scene.

"Arm wrestle you for a piece."

I turned around, startled by the unique request. It came from a guy standing behind me wearing a fedora and decked out in lip, nose, and eyebrow piercings.

"Excuse me?" I said.

He thought for a moment, then tried again. "That just sounded rude, didn't it? Gum. I meant gum."

If he was trying to hit on me, it certainly wasn't working, although he did have a great smile and dimples I wanted to curl up in.

"What if I win?" I replied.

"Win what?"

"Arm wrestling."

He appeared genuinely stumped someone would call him out on his challenge.

"Never thought about that. Make it two out of three?"

I laughed and reached into my purse to take out a pack of gum and offered it to him.

He looked at the pack. "Beemans. That's really going old school."

"Best gum ever."

He took two pieces, leaving me with one. Greedy bastard, I thought.

"Forgive me, but I have to take two. If I only take one, I'll just wind up swallowing it."

"Might as well take 'em all then because I'll do the same."

He smiled and took the remaining piece.

"Thanks," he said, extending his hand. "Finch Redeker."

Finch??? Was this some sick fucking joke? I started to get horrible flashbacks of that uncle who used to drill me on state birds. Life couldn't be that cruel, could it?

I shook his hand, a solid grip, which was always a good sign. I put a lot of stock in someone's handshake. Strong meant confident, while a dead fish meant flee.

"Emma Connolly."

He held eye contact for just the right amount of time, too, falling safely between the lines of the no-sale, shy guy and the creep who skeeved you out.

"Finch, huh?" I teased. "You got a sister named Robin?"

He looked at me with a startled expression. "You know her?"

"I was joking. You do?"

He scrunched up his face and shook his head.

"I want my gum back," I demanded.

He hurriedly unwrapped the pieces and shoved them in his mouth.

I squinted at him. "Duly noted," I warned.

The sound of sharp handclapping suddenly cut through the buzz. A man in his sixties emerged from the crowd.

"Good evening, ladies and gentlemen. My name is Grieg and I will be your instructor. Please, let us move inside," he said with a crisp Germanic accent.

Everyone followed him into the gallery, where there was an avant-garde painting exhibition.

"Look all around you. This is art. I want you to smell it, feel it, breathe it. Let it consume you. Because for most of you this is as close as you'll ever come to being an artist. You may ask yourself, why am I so mean? I am not mean, just honest. And that is the first lesson in becoming an artist. You must be true to yourself. Come, this way!"

We entered a large studio in back that was filled with wooden easels. Proving old habits die hard, I immediately sought out the furthest station from the front. My newfound gum pilferer set up next to me. It was rather presumptive of him, but I dug it.

As the other students set up their pads on their easels, some began to unpack their pencil kits. This caused Grieg to sharply bark out, "Stop! Do not touch your drawing pencils. Put them back!"

People returned their pencils to the cases, a little spooked at the ferocity of this Teutonic tyrant.

"And why do I say that? Because you are not prepared to initiate them. First you must answer questions."

Finch leaned over to me. "The brochure didn't say dick about a pop quiz."

Grieg continued his role as grand inquisitor as he surveyed the room.

"The pad in front of you. What does it remind you of? Anyone?"

He searched for hands and, finding none, zeroed in on Finch.

"You, sir."

"Me?" said a surprised Finch.

"Yes. What does that white pad represent to you?"

Finch thought for a moment, then offered up a gem. "My smile?"

This cracked the whole room up, but Grieg was not amused.

"I'll tell you what it represents. It represents your soul."

"That was my second choice," said Finch, clearly not knowing when to quit.

That got even a bigger laugh from the class as Grieg's face flushed.

"Ah, how lucky we are to have Mr. Funnyman in our presence! Oh please, sir, do entertain us."

Everyone turned to stare at Finch, who by now was looking a little uncomfortable. "Well, I haven't rehearsed, so I'd really be kind of winging it..."

"Then I suggest you listen. And that goes for all of you because you must ask yourself, do you want to be an artist? If so, you'd know then that the blank pad is like the soul at birth. Empty and unformed, but it is through your hands, however, that you will give it meaning and life."

Finch looked at me and deadpanned, "My man is deep."

The rest of the class consisted of us just sitting in front of our drawing pads and staring at them, while Grieg patrolled the room.

I shit you not.

It was like some transcendental meditation session, and one of the most baffling things I'd ever done. Much like my life, there was absolutely no point to it.

After class, Finch and I went over to a nearby cafe, where we ordered up a couple of espressos. He paid, despite actually winning a brief round of rock, paper, scissors to see who was going to pick up the tab. Chivalry was always nice but not a deal breaker, unless the guy was a total tool, and trust me, I'd dated a whole fucking shed full of them.

Finch came over to the couch and handed me my cup. "One espresso macchiato," he said.

"Thanks."

He also set down a plate with a giant peanut butter cookie on it, each of us breaking off a piece, leaving one.

Finch sat across from me and shook his head. "Well, that certainly was different. Who knows, maybe next week we'll actually get to draw something."

"The guy's a freak."

"Yeah, like this mashup of Freud and Hitler, but without the insouciant charm."

"Please, no $10 words. My brain's fried," I begged.

"Sorry, it's habitude."

"Why's that?"

"I'm a writer. Actually, I'm a blogger, but I want to be a writer when I grow up."

Okay, I was intrigued, not to mention a total sucker for the creative types. "What do you blog about?"

"The local scene. I'm just sort of a social gadfly."

He took out his cellphone and showed me a webpage blog with his picture, and an article entitled "Broad Shoulders and Narrow Minds."

"Here. This is the most recent in my *oeuvre*. I really don't have anything to say, yet I do it with such brilliant style."

"And does blogging pay all the bills?"

"Well, I have three roommates and should have my student loans paid off in forty-two years. You tell me."

"Where'd you go to college?"

"DePaul. Got my BA in creative writing. What about you? Where'd you go to school?"

"The Arts Institute."

"No way! One of my old roomies went there. Loved it."

I gracefully pivoted off the subject before messy explanations needed to be doled out.

"What made you want to be a writer?"

"Because I got kicked out of med school for stealing bodies."

I stopped mid-sip and stared at him. He was certainly unique, but it was all right, I could hang.

"So, after you sold off the body parts for coffee money, what made you want to become a writer?" I said, not missing a beat.

Finch smiled, most likely impressed by my ability to match his bullshit shot-for-shot.

"Nelson Algren."

"Who's that?"

"Only the greatest writer ever about the Chicago underclass. Made Bukowski look like Dr. Seuss. I started reading his stuff in college and I was hooked. I knew what I had to do with the rest of my life."

"I will definitely put him on my reading list," I promised.

We both looked down at the remaining cookie piece, then at each other. Without a word being said, we lunged for it at the same time, with me ripping the piece away before he could grab it.

"Savage," he said. "Let me ask you something, what made you take the class?"

"I just thought I'd try it and see."

"See what?"

He had me on that one. Christ, what was the right answer?

"I'm not sure," I said, a weak response to be sure, and well below my usual incendiary ripostes.

"You hate your life too, huh?"

"I didn't say that."

"Didn't have to. The people who take these types of classes have usually reached an emotional stagnation in their lives."

His knack for sizing up a situation was very impressive. Not that I was going to let him know that.

"Gee, thanks. Are you always this judgmental?"

"Nope, just an exemplary judge of character. Look, I freely admit I'm a creative dilettante with no sense of direction."

"Sounds encouraging," I retorted.

"What do you do for a living? Wait, let me guess."

He stared intently at me, then leaned back, having arrived at an answer.

"I'd say either accounting or sales owing to that fluorescent office pallor you have."

"Okay, now I have a question."

"Go."

"Do you know if espresso is tough to get out of leather?"

"No idea. Why?"

I nodded toward the jacket Finch was wearing. "Because we're about to find out."

"Oh no, please don't take any of the shit I say personally. It's just how I am. My high school senior class voted me 'Most Likely to Get Shot.'"

I burst out laughing, almost dousing my skirt in coffee.

"Sales," I answered.

"What?"

"I work in sales."

"Yes!! You buy the next round," Finch exalted as he got up to do the goofiest victory dance.

As we walked out of the cafe and down the street, two thoughts crossed my mind. First, there was no denying that Finch was a helluva good time. He was smart, funny, and interesting-looking. The other was it was way too soon to even think about anything else, as I was still wearing the parka from the nuclear winter that Aaron had set off.

I wasn't the type that thought the best way to get over a failed relationship was to jump into a new one. That was pure masochism. When I was in my early teens, I went horseback riding and was thrown off the mount. My instructor said the only way to get over the trauma was to immediately get back on, so I did.

Guess what? Fucker threw me again.

There wasn't going to be a third time, but I use that to illustrate my point that smart money always said screw conventional thinking. Who'd want to subscribe to anything with the word 'conventional' in it anyway? Which probably explained why my next thought drifted to wondering if Finch had all these piercings, did he also have the Prince Albert thing going on?

That's about as close as I came to linear thinking.

"I have to ask. What's with all the piercings? Why so many?" I quizzed him.

"I just think the body is an ever-evolving work of art and this is how I choose to decorate it."

"There's that word again."

"What word?"

"'Evolving.' Never mind."

A silence passed between us, as somewhere a little red devil was poking me with a trident to ask about whether he had any of the Royal Family visiting down below. I banished the goblin and returned to more meaningful conversation.

"So..." I vamped.

"She said with an awkward pause. Are you showing up next week?"

"Hey, I paid for the course. I want my $39 worth."

"Plus supplies," Finch added.

"Plus supplies."

Finch stopped in front of a beat-up old black Camaro.

"Well, this is me. Can I give you a ride to your car?"

"I'm just right across the street," I said, pointing to my maroon Mini Cooper.

"Uh oh, you are aware of what they say about women who drive Minis?"

"What?"

"Small car, small...well, you know."

Sonofabitch, he was leaving that door wide open! I chose not to take the bait.

Finch climbed into his eyesore of a car and fired up the engine. The sound was godawful. I stared at the car and shook my head.

"I bet this thing violates at least a dozen EPA regulations."

"That's okay. I'm a crime against humanity myself," he winked. "See you next week, Emma. Stay out of jail."

He gunned the engine and peeled out.

Somehow that winter was starting to get a little warmer.

There are three things that you must choose carefully in life, without exception.

Your friends.

Your romantic interests.

And your weed dealer.

I was great at one of them.

I had first met Bolan Kroeger when I was at the Arts Institute, where he had a gift for scoring outstanding bud. His parents had named him after a seventies glam rocker, and he took it to heart, being cocky as all hell. Some people can get away with it, some can't, but Bolan made everyone fall in love with him. He had that BDE before it even became a thing.

I think I was one of the few girls in his orbit that never slept with him, although he did look like he'd be at home modeling for Abercrombie.

Since Illinois went green regarding legalizing pot, Bolan knew his run would eventually end. In the meantime, however, he'd managed to sock away a small fortune from selling, mostly in municipal bonds and tech stocks.

In an odd way, he was also an alter ego to me. He had made it as far as his senior year before he quit, citing burnout. He majored in sculpture, and I was bummed when he dropped out because I thought his stuff was remarkable.

Say what you want, but I think there's a place in the world for ganja-dealing sculptors, but to each his own.

We'd meet up at his condo overlooking Lakeshore East Park and I'd stay for about an hour, shooting the shit and talking about the past a lot.

I came over on a Friday to pick up some supplies for the weekend, and I noticed he was a little down. Bolan was usually high energy, but for some reason, it'd been put on mute.

We sat at the kitchen table as he parceled out the goods.

"Now, this has the frosty trichomes you like, and it's packed with lots of red hairs," he intoned in a voice that sounded like he was hosting an insurance seminar.

"Bolan, what's wrong?" I asked.

He paused for a minute, and I waited for him to come out with some terrible, life-altering pronouncement. I prepped myself for the worst.

"I turned twenty-eight the other day," he finally said quietly.

"Why didn't you tell me? I would've taken you out," I said, totally annoyed.

"Didn't feel like it. I pretty much just sat home."

"With all the friends you have, you chose to sit home?" I was astonished. When we hung out in school, he was king of the social butterflies. How big? We're talking monarch.

"Yeah. I kind of just sat here taking stock."

"And?"

"I'm basic," he concluded.

"Dude, you're anything but basic."

On those rare occasions when I broke out the word 'dude,' that meant I was serious as a fucking stroke.

He pulled at his shirt. "What is this?"

"Is that a trick question?"

"A hemp shirt. It's Friday and I'm wearing cargo shorts and a fucking hemp shirt."

"So what?"

He reached over to the counter and grabbed a bottle of vitamins.

"Fish oil. I'm twenty-eight and I'm taking fish oil."

I was completely at a loss what to do. Plainly this was a serious problem to him, but I found it beyond ridiculous.

He grabbed his sunglasses from around his neck and held them out.
"I've got my sunglasses on a lanyard!"

I couldn't take this anymore and started laughing.

"No, really. You know Paulino's over in Streeterville?" he asked.

"Yeah."

"A couple of buddies and me went over there last week and guess what I got? Chicken parm. I always get the fucking chicken parm!"

"Bolan, I don't think these are really substantial problems."

"They are to me."

"Okay, okay," I said reassuringly. Everyone had their own demons, I guess.

"And I took a side hustle and made it my life."

"But look where you live. You don't have to answer to anybody. You got cash."

"Yeah, but I've got regrets. I'm too young for that shit," he said. "And I shouldn't have dropped out."

Whoa, for some reason he just dumped a truckload of reality into his otherwise hilarious dissertation. In all the time I'd known him, I'd never seen Bolan even be the slightest bit introspective. That's how I knew this was some heavy-ass baggage he was dragging around.

He got up and went to the refrigerator. "You want something to drink?"

"Sure, what do you got?"

He opened the door and let out a yell. He turned around holding a can.

"See? Craft beer. Basic as fuck."

"I'll just have water, thanks." He walked over and handed me a bottle.

"I don't know, maybe I'm wrong. You left and seem to be doing okay," Bolan said.

Oh Christ, please don't use me as a measuring stick, I silently bellowed. I was more lost than Atlantis.

I gestured so-so, praying he'd let it drop at that.

"Why don't you get back into sculpting?" I suggested.

"What for?"

"Because you were great at it."

Bolan waved off my suggestion. "Nah."

It was obvious he felt that ship had already sailed and had been boarded by Somali pirates. Nothing I said was going to change that.

Bolan looked around his clinically perfect condo.

"But I still got Callie," he said as he smiled at a large marble sculpture of a woman's torso in the corner.

He had made that while at school and even won a couple of awards for it.

It was gorgeous, but I don't know if I'd have the courage to look at something every day that was a constant reminder of what I wasn't anymore.

Six

A nother day at the widget factory found me drifting as usual. Hey, I was dealing with a lot of shit here, what with my usual financial woes, the whole apartment thing, and the fact that I had just met an intriguing guy. While my mind tried to compartmentalize each issue, I doodled away on a yellow legal pad.

An uncommonly chipper Tami came over and sat down next to me.

"What's up, Em?"

I stopped doodling and picked up the call sheet.

"Oh hey, Tami. Just fighting the good fight."

"How about we get lunch today?"

"What's the catch?" I said suspiciously.

"No catch. Don't be so cynical. We're buds."

I hoped she wasn't going to bring up the whole nose stud thing again. She hadn't mentioned it for a while, and I, being the ever-obedient employee, had completely ignored the request.

Of course, if they really wanted it, they could take it.

FROM MY COLD, DEAD NOSE!

Tami and I hit up Jee's Spot for lunch, and as luck would have it, I even got the same terrible waiter, but at least he got my order right this time. I looked around the place and shook my head.

"God, this place brings back some bad memories."

"How come?" Tami asked.

"This is where Aaron broke up with me."

Tami just nodded and looked down at her plate, where she was being surgical with her Peking duck.

"Then you're really going to hate this place," she said.

"Why's that?"

"Because I've got to fire you."

I stopped eating and stared at Tami with a dazed expression. I don't know why I should've been so surprised, though. The last few weeks I'd been walking around wearing a giant "Kick Me" sign on my back, as the world had taken turns jamming a boot up my ass, so this fell perfectly into place. I'm not one to feel sorry for myself, but for fuck's sake, wasn't there anyone else life could've picked on? No trust fund babies that needed a good thrashing?

Before I could even get a word of protest in, Tami began her litany of charges.

"Now before you start going off, it came down from upper management that we've got to cut the fat. And just being real here, Em, you're part of it. Your sales numbers are shit and lately it's like your mind is a million miles away. What would you do if you were in my shoes?"

"Kill myself."

Upon further review, this was probably not the best line to use when trying to fight for your job, but at that point not one fuck was given.

"C'mon now, don't take this personally. You realize how hard this is for me?" said Tami, who seemed genuinely hurt.

Oh, thank God, this was going to be all about her pain! For a moment there I thought my insignificant feelings were going to upset the lunch.

I tossed my fork back onto the plate.

"Yeah, I'm sure the struggle is real."

"Look, if you need a reference, I'm here for you."

"Great. 'Emma is a wonderful toner cartridge salesperson and would be an excellent asset to your firm.'"

"Exactly!"

"Tami, I have no money."

Tami reached into her purse and handed me a $100 bill.

"Here, pay me back when you can."

"You owed me this!!"

"Well, that's even better then. Makes for a fresh start."

If we weren't in a restaurant, I probably would've wound up posing for mugshots the rest of the afternoon, which was why she chose to fire me in a public place.

I couldn't take this anymore. Tami had become a clone for this soulless manufacturing conglomerate, and no matter how much I protested, I was still toast.

I grabbed my purse and got up from the table.

"Enjoy the corporate life, you asshole."

I stormed out, but as I left, I wasn't thinking about being fired. I was debating whether I'd used the right pejorative for an exit line. "Bitch" or "cunt" seemed way too obvious, as both were real low-hanging fruit on the insult tree. In my moment of fury, I just suddenly flashed upon trying something different. But then I started to wonder, can girls be assholes? I think it's a gender-neutral term, if you ask me. I thought about this all the way back to my car, probably because it kept my mind off the larger, more terrifying reality which was I had now completely bottomed out.

I'll spare you most of the gory deets, but I sat in my Mini and cried for an hour, using napkins, my sleeve, and even a maxi pad that I had stashed. I hadn't been fired from a job since my early twenties, when I got shit-canned from working at a tanning salon because I refused to tan. It was the dead of a Chicago winter, and I'm so white I glow in the dark to begin with, so everyone would've known it was fake. Not to mention the fact that it was probably unhealthy too. Thinking back, why the fuck did they even hire me?

It didn't matter anyway, and now neither did this job.

I came home in a rage, slammed the door, and hurled my keys across the living room. I had no idea what my next move would be outside of guzzling adult beverages to try and calm my jangled nerves.

I pulled a bottle out of the wine rack and sat down on the couch, popped the cork, and started on a one-way ticket to Drown Town.

"You're home early."

I was so pissed, I couldn't even bother to be surprised anymore that Mr. Spangler had returned.

"And great, now you're back," I seethed. I didn't even turn around to look at him.

"I would be remiss in not asking if something's wrong."

"I got fired."

"What for?"

"Because I couldn't force overpriced junk on people who didn't want it. I'm dead."

Okay, I may be insensitive at times, but that was just completely tone deaf the moment it escaped my mouth. I turned to see him sitting in a chair, looking on in concern.

"No offense," I apologized.

"None taken."

I returned to my bottle.

"You do realize this isn't a bad thing that's happened?" he said optimistically.

I spun around, indignant at such a suggestion. "Are you insane? I'm broke."

"And that's even better news. This is exactly what you need."

"Will you please go away so I can get completely obliterated?"

He got up from the chair and strolled over in front of me, reminiscent of the way he used to stand before us in class.

"Some of the greatest talents have flourished best out of hardship. Schubert composed brilliant symphonies while wracked with syphilis, Van Gogh created masterpieces even though insane, Michelangelo was nearly blind when he painted the Sistine Chapel."

I put the bottle down. Since he wasn't going to allow me to get trashed in peace, I had to confront his logic head-on.

"So, basically what you're saying is become a man, get totally fucked up, and I'll be good to go?"

"I think you're missing the point."

"Wouldn't be the first time."

Having no desire to continue this debate, I got up to head to the privacy of my bedroom. I stopped along the way to point to the sign on the wall.

"I saw your sign. Of course, I'll respect your wishes," Mr. Spangler nodded.

I took a few steps down the hall, then walked back into the living room.

"Tell me, do you haunt any of your other ex-students?"

Mr. Spangler looked genuinely taken aback at my question. "Is that what you think I'm doing?"

"Well, isn't it?"

"The answer is no."

"Great. I win the spectral lottery then. Yay me!" I clapped back.

I've been told by ex-boyfriends that I could sleep through anything: lightning, earthquakes, plane crashes. Someone even cracked that if I ever gave birth, I'd probably sleep through delivery. True dat, because once my head hits that pillow, off to fields of delta waves I go. That's why I was so surprised when I heard the noise and bolted upright, like someone had zapped me with 2000 volts.

A loud, sorrowful wailing was coming from somewhere inside the apartment.

I jumped out of bed, still a little disoriented and wondering if it was just my imagination playing exquisite mind tricks on me.

Then it happened again. Jesus, Mary, and Jerry, what the fuck was going on?

As I slowly walked down the hall, I could now hear "Champagne Supernova" by Oasis coming from the living room.

I came into the darkened room and flipped on the light switch. Mr. Spangler sat at the dining room table with his eyes closed and a beatific look on his face.

"Did you hear that?" I gasped.

He held up a finger, waiting for the song to finish before he opened his eyes to look at me.

"Hear what?"

"That noise."

"You mean that loud, mournful wailing? Oh, that'd be me."

I was livid. I wanted to throw something at him.

"Are you insane?"

"I figured since I am 'haunting' you, as you say, I might as well give you the full spectacle."

I sniffed the air. Hang on, I also smelled reefer.

"And why does the place smell like weed? Have you been smoking out?"

"Miss Connolly, have you any idea how absurd that sounds?"

"Yeah, I stopped using logic the moment you showed up."

I normally had a fairly long fuse, but no more. I was through with this spook show and wanted something done about it right fucking *now*.

"That's it. I'm calling the...shit, I don't know who I'm calling, but I'm calling someone."

I paced back and forth trying to formulate a plan of action and must've looked like a complete fool while doing it.

"Can I ask you something, Miss Connolly?"

I stopped pacing as I realized there was nothing I could do. I looked at Mr. Spangler with utter resignation.

"Sure. I don't have a job to get up for anymore. Let's talk!" I snarked.

I hopped up on a stool. I was all ears.

"Do you miss painting?"

Whoa. I usually can bat back anything thrown in my face with vicious skill, but I sure wasn't expecting that. Totally threw me for a loop and stung like a bitch.

"I haven't really thought about it," I tossed out casually.

This garnered a dubious look from Mr. Spangler, as I was now forced to play defense, a position I had always loathed.

"You think I'm lying?" I said.

"What's that saying? 'The most hurtful lies are the ones we tell ourselves.'"

I sagged and shook my head, "Please, it's four in the morning. Don't go all Dr. Phil on me. I'm too tired."

Mr. Spangler just continued to stare at me. Both of us knew this was sub-standard bilge I was serving up. Certainly not my usual USDA prime grade. He had called me on my shit and now I was just looking for a semi-graceful way out.

"What? All right, great. I'll paint you something. Will that get you to leave? Unfreakinbelievable."

I hopped off the stool and walked into the kitchen.

"Yes," he answered simply.

"Yes what?"

"I accept your offer."

I stopped in my tracks. Did I just hear this right? I turned around and walked back toward him.

"Really? Like, no bullshit?"

"You have my word. Pick a number."

"Why?"

"Please, just humor me. Pick a number between one and ten."

"Okay, eight," I sighed.

"Eight it is then. In exchange for my leaving, you create eight paintings. Acrylic, watercolor, doesn't matter. You do that, and I will disappear forever."

I was furious with myself. I knew I should've picked three, but I was hung up on that whole infinity thing, eight sideways, never mind. It didn't matter though, there was an exit strategy now in play.

"Look, what's this going to prove anyway?" I argued.

"It'll prove once and for all that there's still a creative spark alive inside you. Circumstance has just buried it."

"Swell, I'll give it a Viking funeral."

"By the way, how do you like those drawing classes?"

"How did you know I'm doing that?" I said, suspicious as all hell.

Mr. Spangler nodded over to my drawing pad and pencil kit that sat on the table.

"Oh. You don't follow me around, do you, because that'd be a major ick factor. As if this isn't fucked up enough to begin with," I said.

"Of course I don't."

"Respect," I affirmed, and pumped my arm mockingly.

I walked over to the living room closet, stepped inside, and closed the door.

Two can play at this, I thought.

Actually, it was to get my stash jar, which at one point, I had completely covered in Christmas tree stickers. Why? Like I remember? I probably did it when I was smoking gas, but it certainly did keep things festive-looking throughout the year. I glanced inside. Everything seemed okay, but who knows if he pinched a few buds for himself. I took the jar and walked back out.

Crossing the living room, I gave Mr. Spangler a hard stare. I headed back to the bedroom with my arms wrapped tightly around the jar, just like a mother bear protecting her cub.

I wandered the aisles of the art supply store, stuffing my cart with canvases, brushes, tarps, and paints. It felt good to be among the tools of the trade again, even if I had deserted them long ago for browner pastures. My main concern was whether I could be moved by the creative spirit once more. I knew all this was for a completely ludicrous reason, but no matter what I'd ever done in life, I always wanted to put my best effort forward.

Okay, let me revise that, because my life choices over the past ten years completely invalidated that last comment. Whenever I had applied my talents to something, I always strived to be the best. There, better?

I rolled up to the checkout counter, where the clerk looked at my haul and shook his head.

"You planning on starting your own wing at the MCA?"

"Nope, just trying to get a ghost to leave," I said without thinking.

He gave me an unsure look, but I just looked right back him.

"What?"

"Whatever," he said as he rang me up.

I had rented a U-Haul van for my shopping spree and crammed it all inside. Everything total, including van rental, came to about $300, but I was determined to regain control of my life and apartment once again.

Back home, I stared at the living room. How was I going to make this happen? I hated to use the term Feng Shui because it made me sound like some chakra-loving poseur who only bought import furniture, but the couches, TV, tables, and chairs all needed to be rearranged to give me some working room. I spent the next hour moving things out of the way, draping tarps, setting up easels, and spreading out paints and brushes. I finally finished and stood looking at the completely revamped living room. So much for hosting the spring cotillion.

Mr. Spangler came up beside me and nodded his approval.

"Congratulations, Miss Connolly, you've turned this place into a first-class atelier. I must say, this is quite exceptional."

"I've done something completely nuts is what I've done."

"Inspired," he countered.

I made up a canvas, then proceeded to squeeze the paints onto a palette. I loved using acrylics because of the texture and the fact that I didn't have to prime the canvas before using them. Some snobs saw oils as a "purer" form of painting, but go tell that to Warhol, Lichtenstein, and Hockney, fuckos. I had zero tolerance when it came to pretension. Maybe that's why I ultimately gave up on painting, because subconsciously I knew I would be subject to the whims and affectations of people who couldn't beat me in a knife fight.

So there I was, poised with brush in hand and ready for action, the first time I would've touched a canvas in years.

And then something happened. Actually, nothing happened. I stared at the canvas, paralyzed by indecision at how to start. I could've doubled as a statue in Lincoln Park for the pigeons to shit on, I was that locked up.

I let out a frustrated sigh and put the brush down. Mr. Spangler, who was sitting on the couch working a sudoku puzzle, looked over at me.

"Something wrong?"

"This is ridiculous. I can't do this." I got up and stepped back from the canvas.

"And why's that?"

"I have no idea."

"Would it be better if I wasn't here while you painted?"

I paused and thought for a moment. Is that what it was?

"I don't know. Maybe. Yeah."

"All right then."

He got up from the couch and walked over to the living room closet again. He stepped inside and closed the door behind him.

With that mental obstacle out of the way, I picked up the brush to resume my attempt. Being the semi-neurotic I was, though, soon I had a new problem. My attention was split between the canvas in front of me and the closet door.

Curiosity ultimately won out, as I walked over and yanked open the door.

Mr. Spangler stood inside, hands folded in front of him.

"You do realize this closet doesn't lead anywhere? I just do this for dramatic effect," he said.

After killing an hour or so feeding my YouTube addiction (mostly Russian car crashes), as well as keeping numerous online retailers flush, my awe-inspiring gift for procrastination finally crumbled under the weight of its own bloat.

Let's just do this. Lean the fuck in, I thought.

Brush back in hand, I began to attack the canvas and within minutes it all came flooding back: scumbling, flat wash, cross-hatching. All the techniques that had carried me when I was younger had returned to action.

Once learned, there are certain muscle memory skills that will never desert you throughout your life. Riding a bike, playing an instrument, and fucking are all prime examples of this. It's just indisputable scientific fact. I used to think swimming was another one, but a few years ago I almost drowned at Oak Street Beach, totally wasting a year of community pool swimming lessons and forever invalidating my Tadpole Certificate I earned when I was nine.

My parents would've been so ashamed had they known.

I had decided to paint a surrealistic landscape composed entirely of various *fromages* in different forms of decay. Where did the idea come from? Who the fuck knows. Where does any idea come from? A lot of artists will tell you things just pop in their head fully formed. I think this was an image that had been sitting somewhere deep in the recesses of my brain for a long time. Believe it or not, I never blazed up before I painted. Hard to comprehend, huh? To me, the purest visions always seemed to come to me when I was fully lucid. I was surprised at how fast I was able to do the majority of the painting, finally stopping around dinnertime because of a previous engagement.

Yes, I was going back under the caustic tutelage of Grieg. Not that I really needed the course anymore, but certain unforeseen circumstances had turned it into a desirable destination.

Seven

Back in drawing class we finally got turned loose and everyone was doing the beginning art student stuff, mostly fruits and objects. Never one to follow suit, I sketched two bananas with faces and arms that were provocatively peeling each other. Relatively tame for me, but still with enough of a twist.

I glanced over at Finch's pad and saw he was drawing a vase that had been set in front of him, but he'd decided to add a few flourishes, namely serpentine vines spilling out of the vase that choked a screaming face.

It was something I would've done.

"You need help," I said.

"Hey, I draw what I see."

"Yes, and it scares me."

From up front, Grieg's voice called out sharply. "No talking! You do not interrupt the creative process!"

Finch playfully rapped me on the hand with his pencil for my transgression.

Grieg wandered among the students, shaking his head as he surveyed everyone's work.

"Ghastly. Dreadful. Insipid. What is wrong with you people? Where is the passion? I am not feeling this at all. You disappoint me."

I'm sorry, wasn't there supposed to be no talking for fear of disrupting the creative process? And for Christ's sake, people were drawing inanimate objects, what did he expect? How much passion can you muster drawing a friggin' eggplant?

When Grieg had reached the back, he glanced at my drawing with an indifferent shrug.

"Too juvenile," he concluded.

Oh fuck you, Herr Grieg.

As you can see, I took criticism like a boss.

He then stopped to stare at Finch's bizarre drawing and nodded his head.

"Interesting."

On the way out to our cars, I was in full-on tease mode. The non-sexual kind.

"Looks like someone's teacher's pet," I said as I nudged Finch with a shoulder bump.

"Oh please. You think I care about praise from that guy? Now I know for sure what I'm doing is bad. It always is."

I stopped walking and stared at Finch.

"Jeez, I'd like Confidence for $1000, Alex."

"No, it's true. Actually, I'm surprised I've hung with the class this long."

"This long? We've only had two classes, unless I slept through a few."

"What I mean is I tend to bail on things in short order."

"Oh," I stated flatly as my image of Finch disintegrated right before my eyes. I had so hoped I'd found someone to fill in those tiny chasms I sometimes lacked in self-esteem.

"Thanks for the warning," I offered up in full retreat.

"No, no, I don't mean you. I like you."

"For now, but obviously that's subject to change."

Finch walked over and gave me one of his patented semi-crooked smiles, the kind I bragged about to all the girls when we played squash at the country club.

"Seriously, I like your sass."

I did a quick mental re-evaluation of him. Perhaps I had been too hasty in my otherwise unimpeachable judgment. What if we could compensate for each other's deficiencies somehow? Mustn't ever throw the baby out with the bath water, unless it was a really fucking annoying baby.

"Thanks," I said. "That extra 's' saved you a slap."

We looked at each other knowing major alchemy was at work here, but I wasn't making a move and neither was he, which led me to start wondering what his damage was.

"You going home?" he asked.

"Yeah, I guess," I said, trailing off and hoping he'd pick up on my definitive indefinitive.

I wasn't trying to be coy. Oh, all right, I was. I had never been good at these awkward beginnings. What was I supposed to do, hold up a damn mugboard that read "Insert suggestion here"?

And I certainly wasn't going to tell him I needed to get up early for a non-existent job. I didn't want to look like some deadbeat, and my working-class bloodline strictly prohibited lying about employment. We Irish were a prideful bunch.

"Nah, it's too early. There's still plenty of hijinks to be had. Besides, I've got a reputation to uphold."

"Which is what?" I said, taking the bait.

"That I'm the most fun you can have without getting naked."

"My dad said nothing great ever has to advertise."

"Which is usually the case, but there are exceptions. Hang on, I've got an idea."

He pulled out his phone and texted a message. A few moments later a response came back that made Finch smile.

"We're in at Torchlight."

"What's that?"

He motioned me to follow him to his Deathmobile. "C'mon, you'll love it. Are you packing?"

"What?! No."

"That's okay, I am."

I stopped abruptly and refused to take another step until I knew what fate I was being led toward.

"I'm joking," Finch grinned.

"I'm not getting in that thing," I said, motioning to his car. "We'll take mine."

Finch grumbled and turned around.

"Fine. I'm sending you my chiropractor's bill then," he said as he jerked his lanky frame toward my crucible of crunch.

On the way over, I got a quick course in Torchlight's colorful history. It was most notable for being one of Al Capone's favorite haunts during Prohibition and had been open for like a hundred years. Literally. Now it was known mainly for poetry slams, which I wasn't crazy about, but I was in luck as it was big band night. Liquor me up enough, and I'd been known on occasion to break out some of my old swing dance moves.

I just hoped it wasn't one of those bars around town that had been gentrified into oblivion, because I sure dug me some dives.

Once there my fears were put to rest, as from the outside it looked like an old-fashioned neighborhood bar. Finch was friends with the manager, and even though they were packed, he squeezed us in.

Inside, it was dark as sin. Thick leather booths, slightly garish statues, and lots of mirrors. I loved the feel of the place and if I ever opened a bordello, I'd want it to look just like this.

"This is great," I grinned as we pushed through to the busy bar.

"What do you want?" Finch asked.

"A Rob Roy."

Finch looked a bit surprised.

"What, too bougie?" I asked.

"No, I just didn't figure you for that. Thought you'd be more the rum and Coke type."

"Oh, that'll come later. Why, what's your go-to?"

"Always start things off with a Zombie."

A solid choice, I thought. You learned a lot about a guy when he got his drink on. If he ordered domestic beer or shots, forget it. He just wanted to get fucked up fast and without shame. Pass. Same for Jäger and margaritas, which totally screamed ex–frat boy. Wine and martinis were classy, but usually meant a boring bastard. Drinks that sprouted chest follicles were the lure for me.

Finch turned to the bartender, a short, beefy man who resembled the missing link.

"Can I please get a Rob Roy and a Zombie?"

The bartender looked at me and nodded. "Let me see your I.D."

"You're joking." I was dumbstruck. I hadn't been carded in forever, which I guess meant I should've taken the request as a compliment.

"Absolutely. I do stand-up behind the bar here five nights a week," he said, stone-faced.

I didn't know whether to laugh or be mad, so naturally I laughed.

I tend to do that when confronted. Makes for a big hit when pulled over by the police.

I shook my head, took out my license, and handed it to him.

He glanced at it for a moment and cracked a smile. "A leapling."

"Yeah, how'd you know?" I said.

He pointed to my birthday. "Dead giveaway."

"No, I mean how do you know what it is?"

"You're looking at one."

"No way," I beamed.

"Yep."

Finch was totally lost as to what was going on. "Someone want to fill me in?"

"Leaplings are people born on February 29th. We're special," I winked at Finch.

The bartender handed me my license back and offered a handshake. "I'm Brandyn. Nice to meet a fellow club member. I'll get your drinks."

I noticed Finch was furiously typing on his phone, then started reading.

"'Leaplings make up 0.0575 percent of the population. Notable people born on February 29th include Tony Robbins, Aileen Wuornos, and Richard Ramirez, better known as 'The Night Stalker.'"

"Yeah, it's a real popular day for serial killers."

"When do you celebrate?" Finch asked.

"Depends. Sometimes it'll be on the 28th or March 1st, or other times people will forget completely."

"Stop right there. No pity party allowed. You're looking at a Christmas Eve baby. Try always having your birthday and Christmas gifts rolled into one."

"You're right. I can't compete with that. You win."

We got our libations and Finch raised his glass in a toast.

"To bad choices and the great stories they make. Cheers."

"*Sláinte.*"

We clinked glasses as Finch looked quizzically at me. "Where's that from?"

"It's Irish."

"Ah, then if we're going all tribal, *Prost*! That's salutations from Deutschland."

"Terrific, we represent the two drunkest tribes on Earth," I said.

"Don't tell the Russians that."

Finch nodded over to a large booth across the way.

"You see that? That was always Capone's booth. He sat there because he had a clear view of both the front and back doors. He'd have guys stationed all over, and if they got a tip the police were coming, it'd be relayed to Capone so he could duck out in time behind the false wall in back of the booth."

I must say, I was quite impressed with Finch's encyclopedic knowledge of syphilitic, murderous Chicago crime lords. That's something you just don't find every day.

"How do you know all this?"

"Because if you're going to write about the city, you better do extensive research and know its history. It's also on that plaque above the booth."

The rest of the night was a blur of non-stop intoxication, interspersed with my trying to teach Finch the basics of swing dancing on a floor smaller than an airplane toilet. He was a quick learn, although he kept peppering it with typical white guy dance moves, which I found funny.

And by the end of the night, we wound up sleeping together.

But not how you think.

The sound of a trash truck backing up rousted me from my slumber, as I awoke to find Finch and myself somehow back in my car in the parking lot across from the bar. When they list the world's greatest unsolved mysteries, we're talking Stonehenge, the Bermuda Triangle, and the Black Dahlia, I do hope they'll leave room for how we wound up here, because there was absolutely no recollection on my end.

Finch's face was smooshed against the door, his body more contorted than Stephen Hawking playing Twister. I thought I was going to need the Jaws of Life to help pry him out.

I debated whether to wake him and finally decided to give him a gentle poke. He coughed and kept his eyes closed.

"Are we dead?" he asked.

Yes, when you roll up to the Pearly Gates you do it in a Mini Cooper.

"Not by the technical definition," I assured him.

He slowly sat up and tried to get his bearings. "How did I get here?"

"I was hoping you'd fill me in. What's the last thing you remember?"

"My birthday party when I was seven. That's how bad this is."

He moaned as he tried to straighten his body out. He rolled his head over and looked at me.

"What time is it?"

I glanced at my watch, waiting a moment for my eyes to adjust. "7:30."

"Right on time. Can you drive me to St. James Cathedral and just dump me on the doorstep? I'll be there all day praying if you need me."

"For real?"

"No."

Finch suddenly sat upright. Well, as upright as he could get.

"Holy shit, I just noticed. You have different colored eyes."

"No way! When did that happen?" I said mockingly.

"It's kind of subtle, but they definitely are different. One is dark green and the other is dark brown. That is great. What does it mean?"

"It means you're *really* inattentive."

Finch shook his head. "Nah. A little slow on the uptake sometimes, but you will always get my undivided attention. Does it have any special significance?"

"Native Americans say it means you can see into both heaven and earth at the same time with them. Others say it's proof I'm a witch, or I have a dead twin that's trying to get out."   .

"Forget I asked. I'll stick with it looks great."

I drove Finch back to his vehicular hazard, watching in amusement as he hoisted his body out of the friendly confines of my car.

"Finch, drive safely," I advised.

"Will do. Thanks for the great night. Whatever it was." He gave me a thumbs up, then leaned back in. "Does this technically mean we've slept together?"

"No."

"Didn't think so," he nodded in agreement.

He closed the door and waved goodbye.

It had been a few years since I'd done the Walk of Shame, but that was exactly what happened when I dragged my hungover ass home at 8 a.m., still dressed in last night's clothes.

I wasn't proud about it, but so be it. I had a great time, at least what I could remember of the night before, and the more I thought about things, I was okay with what happened. I needed to let off a little steam from all the frustrations that'd been stacking up like firewood in my life. A little drink and dance, fine, a lot of drink, had sure hit the sweet spot.

I entered an empty apartment with no sign of Mr. Spangler anywhere. Of course, this didn't mean a thing, as he was liable to pop up unannounced at virtually anytime. It did get me to wonder about where he went to when he wasn't at my place. It's not like he had errands to run.

I slithered into bed, sleeping until 2 p.m., which made me mad because I had wasted a perfectly good day. Whenever I did shit like this, to borrow one of my dad's old phrases, I felt as useless as the 'g' in phlegm and twice as ugly.

Later in the afternoon, I wound up hunched over my laptop looking at job board sites. Mr. Spangler had returned and sat next to me with his arms crossed in disapproval.

"God, there's nothing but garbage on here," I groused.

"I told you that you're not going to find anything."

I shut the laptop in frustration. "Well, then it's back to webcam sex."

He gave me a scolding look.

"Just kidding. I'd never abandon stripping," I reassured him.

"Let me ask you. What are you equipped to do? What are your skills?"

I drew a complete blank, stumped for a substantive answer.

My advice to the world is if you ever reach the tender age of twenty-seven and can't answer that question, feel free to break the glass and pull the red lever.

You have a fucking emergency.

"I've been working McJobs for so long I can't even come up with a good snarky answer. Can I get back to you on that one?"

"I know the answer," said Mr. Spangler.

I got up and grabbed my keys. "Don't start," I warned.

"Are you forgetting our deal?"

"Are you forgetting I have rent to pay?"

And with that I left the apartment in hopes of finding some gainful means of employment.

If you've ever been to a recruitment agency, you'll know it's exactly like the DMV, only minus the glamour. They're usually populated by people who look like they're straight out of a David Lynch film, with wait times that approach a millennium, even with an appointment.

I was seated in the holding area, clutching my clipboard while I waited to be called by the recruiter. Next to me was a hygienically challenged man who couldn't stop his leg from shaking. Across the way was a girl about my age who was crying for some unknown reason and a middle-aged man who kept staring at me. At least I think he was. He had a literal wandering eye that would float back and forth like some endless tennis volley.

"Emma Connolly?"

I looked up to see an overly peppy man in his forties standing in the doorway.

"Right here," I said.

"Hi, I'm Carl, and I'll be your recruitment advisor. How are you today?"

"I'm fine."

"Fantastic. Let's go get you a job, shall we?"

"Great."

For some reason, our banal banter caused the girl to start crying even harder.

I got up and joined Carl as he looked over at her.

"Is she okay?" he quietly asked me.

"Probably not," I said.

Carl offered her a conciliatory smile. "We'll get someone in here right away."

"I'm fine," she sniffled.

I'd hate to see what her concept of miserable was then.

As I followed Carl out of the room, I couldn't help but take a parting glance back at the waiting room, content in knowing that our future work force was in good hands.

Sitting at Carl's desk, I noticed his cubicle wall was plastered with cloyingly cute animal pictures, while a framed photo of him with Oprah sat next to his computer.

"When did you meet Oprah?" I asked, trying to make small talk.

"I didn't."

"I just asked because I saw the picture."

He looked at the photo and laughed. "Oh that. I have no idea where this came from," he said dismissively.

Ohhhkay, I thought, and let it drop. After all, who was I to question workplace adornments, what with my fake travelogue that I used to put up.

He looked over my resume, nodding his head and making a lot of "mmhmm" sounds.

"So, you've worked in sales for the last six years. That's good, that's good. It's always nice when you have someone who can get along well with the public."

He motioned me to lean closer. "You'd be surprised how many people suck at it."

He suddenly broke into this braying laugh, forceful enough that I could smell his stank breath. He typed some data into the computer and notated the results.

"Hmm, it's too bad you don't have a background in the arts."

I immediately perked up. "Actually, I do."

My answer caused Carl to become quite animated. His eyes lit up like Vegas on New Year's Eve. "Really? Me too! I used to play violin in middle school."

"That's great," I said, feigning interest.

"Yep, my teacher, Miss Khaler, thought I was a natural at it. But she never made me first chair, although I deserved it, and she *knew* it."

Carl's mood suddenly dimmed and he looked off with a vacant stare.

A bad memory had come to play.

He lowered his voice as he tried to offer himself advice. "Come on. Find the happy place."

A pall had suddenly descended over the interview. I realized it was up to me to bring him back from whatever dark corner of the universe he was currently visiting.

I cleared my throat. "So, what's the job?"

He drifted back, acting as if nothing had happened. "Oh, right. Well, this is good."

"What?"

"*Very* good," he teased. "Somebody must've known you were coming."

Now it was my turn to be excited, as imaginings ran through my head. I was finally going to be able to do something creative and get paid for it. No more grunt work sucking the marrow from my bones.

Deliverance had finally arrived!

"What is it?" I asked, brimming with anticipation.

"There's an opening for an assistant conductor with the Anchorage Orchestra. They're needed for the winter season."

Did you ever wonder how some people got their jobs? Sure, there was nepotism, although what family would've really wanted to claim Carl?

I just sat and scowled at him. "I am completely unqualified for that."

"Darn," he pouted. "Don't you just love classical music, though? It's so romantic." He returned to his computer to further fuck with my feelings. "Let's see what else there is. Now this is a real good possibility."

"What is?" I asked suspiciously.

"There's an immediate opening for a taekwondo instructor in West Loop."

I felt my blood pressure shoot up to 120 over a billion. "Did you even read my resume?" I snapped.

"It's just a little joke I like to play. There's no such job. I just love saying taekwondo."

I was inches away from grabbing the picture of Oprah and cracking this clown over the head with her.

"Taekwondo. It really gives the tongue a good workout. Try it!"

I'd had enough. "Is there a supervisor I can talk to?" I asked as I looked around the area.

"It's all right. I'll find you something. I'm sure we'll get you a job you'll be just perfect for."

Eight

"Hi, this is Emma Connolly calling from A & J Services. May I speak to whoever orders your janitorial supplies? Whomever. Thank you for correcting my grammar."

And with that inauspicious opening, I began my new job. True to his word, Carl had found me work based on my skills. It just happened to be hawking toilet paraphernalia at a janitorial supply company in the Central Business District, but who was I to complain?

I was employed again.

Gone was my window cubicle, now replaced by penitentiary-gray walls in a honeycomb of similar work stations. Actually, it wasn't as horrible as it sounded. My boss was great, there were a couple of genuinely nice people I worked with, and once you got past the idea of what you were pushing, it became just like any other sales job.

On the downside, I was now making less money than before, but they had a better health plan. That was good because I planned on seeing a therapist every day until I figured out some way to pull out of this nosedive of a life.

Back home I was down for another night of hardcore gaming, even though I had a Netflix queue waiting for me that made the Library of Congress look like a take-out menu. My focus eventually began to drift from the game over to the empty canvasses that sat there waiting for me to bring them to life.

Oh my God, had I somehow allowed Grieg to invade my subconscious? The mere thought of it rocked me to my core.

I'm not sure how it was with other people, but in the past, I had always felt kind of dirty when I wasn't creating. Like I hadn't showered in a couple of weeks.

That feeling had started to creep back again.

I spent the next six hours going non-stop on my third and fourth paintings. I was working fast not because I wanted to meet my agreed quota, but more because something had been knocked loose inside me. I was imbued with the same artistic rush I used to have, where the rest of the world could just go fuck itself, and my focus would be on nothing but the canvas in front of me.

I had also made a complete mess of my living room. I was never the neatest of painters to begin with, but it was a good mess, the kind born out of sheer determination and experimentation. Spills, splashes, and sloshes decorated the floor, my clothes, and my hair. Like a paintball range, but with a bigger palette.

When I finally stopped for the night, I couldn't believe it was almost 2 a.m. When you're in that zone, time just becomes a rumor as hours turn into mere minutes. I wasn't even tired, but I had to be up for work in six hours.

Wonderful, glorious work.

I stood at the kitchen sink cleaning off brushes, extremely content with my output. For some reason, I even had a silly grin on my face.

"You must want me out of here very badly."

I let out a scream and jumped. Mr. Spangler was leaning on the countertop behind me.

"Will you stop doing that? Jesus, announce yourself or something. Like with trumpets or a fucking harp. Anything," I complained.

"I see almost four paintings done. How does it feel?"

"Different, but good."

"It must be invigorating to be using your talents once again."

I shrugged in agreement. Mr. Spangler was right, but I'd always had a hard time admitting when I was wrong. I was dumb that way.

I finished with the brushes and put them in a jar, then turned and looked at him.

"Can I ask you something?"

"Of course."

I paused for a moment, trying to figure out a diplomatic way to ask what I'm sure everyone has ever wanted to know.

"What's it like?"

"What's what like?"

"You know..." I said, trying not to be obvious.

"Sorry, I don't."

"Being..." I hesitated.

"Being what?" Mr. Spangler asked with a look of confusion.

Should I just suck it up and stop being so damn tactful?

"Forget it."

"No, please, speak your mind."

"I mean..." I said as I continued to dance around the point.

Finally, the light bulb went off over Mr. Spangler's head. "Oh, you mean what's it like being...DEAD?" he said, leaning toward me for emphasis, as I started to back up, a little unnerved.

"Well, yeah," I said.

"I knew what you meant. I just wanted to see how long I could draw it out."

I glared at him. From now on, fuck tact.

He paused a moment to think. "I find that I have a lot more time on my hands."

I shook my head in disgust. Here I was trying to have a serious discussion of what to expect, and he was being a wiseass.

"Screw it. Never mind," I said.

I walked into the living room to continue the cleanup.

"I'm not sure what you want me to say," said Mr. Spangler.

"You don't have to say anything," I said as I started to recap the paint tubes.

"You must understand, I'm fairly limited in what I can tell you."

This got my attention. I looked at him, more than a bit mystified.

"What's that supposed to mean?"

"It means I can't really talk about it."

"What, you sign some NDA when you die?" I joked.

"Of sorts."

"Whatever you say. Or don't say."

"There are certain guidelines everyone has to follow."

"Like what?"

He just smiled. No doubt he was adhering to the rules and regulations set forth in Article 1, Section A, Clause 3 of the Civil Code of the Deceased Act. Now, see, if I had chosen pre-law I would've known shit like this.

"I'm just asking, am I going to see my pet dog I had when I was a kid? Am I going to be stuck with my annoying relatives again?"

"I can tell you the reason *why* I can't discuss it," said Mr. Spangler.

"And why's that?"

"Because if everyone knew what awaited them, some, shall we say, might not wait."

"I get it. Well, that's not me, and it's a little fucking dark, but it makes sense."

"I will tell you it's very peaceful. A bit dull at times, perhaps, but overall I have no complaints."

"Really? I was thinking you'd be all pissed. You weren't that old, were you?"

"No, but that trope is true. Age is all relative."

"I guess."

I stashed the empty food containers in the trash bag and dragged it to the front hallway.

"But, yes, initially I was quite mad," confirmed Mr. Spangler.

"Aha! I was right."

"But not for the reasons you'd think. I'd just bought a house, and after I died all that equity wound up going to the state because I didn't have any family."

"You weren't married?"

"Me? God no. And no kids. At least none that I knew of."

"Were you gay?"

Mr. Spangler chuckled and shook his head. "Far from it."

"That's what all the kids in class thought."

"Was it really? That's hilarious."

"Hey, high school kids are morons."

"No, I lived the bachelor's life with a capital 'B.' Which, in hindsight, is probably what killed me."

I stopped what I was doing and took a seat at the counter. He had my undivided attention as I waited for him to spill the tea.

"No way," I said.

"It's true. Drank, smoked, dated women who were bad for me. I might've died relatively young, but I definitely didn't get cheated."

"All right, Rock Star!" I said, leaning over to fist bump him and then pulled back, realizing how absolutely dumb the idea was. "YOLO," I added.

"Excuse me?"

"You only live once."

"Well, twice if you know the right people. And Miss Connolly, since I'm getting things out in the open, I do have a confession to make."

"What?"

"I did appropriate a bit of your stash."

"Shit, I knew it!"

"There's nothing that says we have to give up *all* earthly pleasures."

I hopped off the stool and shook my head.

"Whatever works for you. Good night."

"Good night, Miss Connolly."

I made it about halfway down the hall before "Champagne Supernova" started playing once again, along with the pungent aroma of cannabis back in the air.

I returned to the living room and gave Mr. Spangler a look.

"I had a little left over," he said.

Our weekly class had now reached the figure drawing portion of the course, which naturally put me in a coma. It shut down all imagination, but being a good soldier, I complied. Finch proved pretty adept at drawing people, although he kept needling me to ask Grieg when the nude models were arriving. I swear, sometimes I thought he was the little brother I never had, he could be that maddening.

"How's the new job going?" asked Finch as we packed up for the evening.

I gave him an obvious stare.

"That high on the misery index?" he asked.

"I'm buying more lottery tickets than ever. That tell you something?"

"Yes. You'll never be my financial planner."

I laughed and dropped my sketch pad. Finch bent down to pick it up and hand it back to me.

"Thanks," I said.

Finch gave me a look. You know, *that* look, then swooped in to steal a quick kiss.

Sexy, sweet, and salty. He'd been eating sunflower seeds earlier.

"I forgot that from last week," Finch whispered.

"That's just wrong in so many ways."

"Oh yeah? Name one."

"Okay, starting with the fact he got to see our first kiss."

I nodded toward the front of the room, where Grieg was staring right at us. He shook his head disapprovingly and walked away.

"Ouch. Yeah, that is wrong," Finch grimaced, then turned his attention back to me, a mischievous twinkle in his eye. "First, huh? As in more to come?"

We walked out to our cars in silence while trading fuck me eyes. The attraction had reached critical mass, with the sexual tension so thick you could cut it with a chainsaw, just in case the knife broke.

"So, how are we going to corrupt the rest of the evening?" Finch pondered.

I responded by dropping my sketch pad again, this time on purpose, and backing Finch up against his car. Since he'd already gotten his licks in, it was time for me to step up.

Quid pro fucking quo.

I pressed into him and stood on tiptoes to give him a full-on kiss. The kind he'd remember on a dreary winter night when I was just a fond memory, twenty years on.

I then backed off and smoothed over my smeared lipstick with my thumb. "Not sure," I said.

I've always been a big proponent of PDAs, although to some I knew they were anathema, which I've never understood. I'm not saying be some ho, but if you're not going to share in public what you'd do in private, you have a real disconnect. Excluding the obvious.

Finch seemed pleasantly surprised by my response. "That's not a bad start," he replied.

We must've looked like a couple of horny teens going at it hard and heavy, with me resting against his car. Say what you want about Finch's unorthodox appearance, but fuck, the man sure knew how to kiss. His hands, mouth, and tongue were making me wetter than Seattle in November.

After about five minutes of blissfully denying each other oxygen, we finally came up for air. He leaned over to my ear, gently bit it, then whispered a suggestion.

"How about we go back to your place?"

Suddenly, I felt a bit apprehensive. Not with my current living situation, we weren't. I pulled back a little.

"Let's go to yours," I offered.

"Can't. My roomies are home."

"So?"

"Emma, I live in a loft. There's about as much privacy as a bus terminal. We're having a party soon. Come over and see for yourself."

"It's just that..."

Finch gently squeezed my lips together with his fingers. "No more protestations. Thought is the death of spontaneity." He let go of my lips.

"Who said that?" I asked.

"I did. It's my one original thought and I must guard it fiercely."

"Got it."

"Good," he said, then ducked in one more kiss.

I finally relented and we decided to go back to my place. We made a stop at Portillo's for a take-out dinner, but on the way home, I spent the whole time worrying about what I was going to do.

No way was I going to mention to Finch about what he was possibly walking into, mainly for fear of the reaction I might get. I couldn't imagine anything killing a potential relationship quicker than explaining why the ghost of your high school teacher was making periodic guest appearances in your apartment.

Finch was pretty chill, but that just screamed crazy chick in neon.

It was obvious I had to get in there first and lay down the law to Mr. Spangler.

We parked our cars in the garage and walked the labyrinthian maze you needed to traverse to reach my apartment. I'm sure Finch noticed I seemed a little preoccupied; my mind was having an emergency council meeting.

"You okay?" he gently prodded.

"Me? Yeah. Great. Why?"

God, I was such a horrible liar.

"You've been on radio silence since we left the garage."

"Really? I'm sorry. Just a million things."

I motioned to the hallway leading to my apartment.

"I'm over here."

He opened the hallway door, and as we walked down the faded carpet that was cleaned once every decade, I stopped outside my front door.

"Okay, I didn't plan on this happening. You're going to have to give me a minute."

"What's wrong?"

"I've been doing some painting and the place is a total disaster."

"Doesn't bother me. Try growing up with two brothers in one room."

It was my turn to grab his lips. "Patience," I urged.

I kissed him on the cheek and went into the apartment.

I put the food down on the kitchen counter and looked around.

"Mr. Spangler, where are you?" I called out.

The response came from down the hall. "In the bathroom."

I had two reactions. The first was, huh? Why would he be using the bathroom? The second was he'd broken our agreed-upon line of trust and I was mad.

I stalked down the hall to the bathroom, pausing to take the sign down off the wall. I could just imagine trying to explain that one to Finch.

I found Mr. Spangler on his knees in the bathroom examining the baseboard of the sink.

"What are you doing in here?" I steamed.

"I think you might have an ant problem. I've tracked it down to here. Come have a look."

"No," I said defiantly.

He looked up at me. "What's wrong?"

"You broke our agreement. I feel violated."

"What agreement?" he said as he stood up.

"You agreed not to come past that sign outside on the wall."

"For God's sake, I'm just trying to help."

"Thanks, Orkin Man, but a deal is a deal."

He looked at me and nodded. "You're right and I apologize."

He followed me out into the living room, where I made a half-hearted effort to achieve some semblance of order. The place looked like a Category 5 had hit it, with tarps and supplies strewn about.

"Look, I have someone waiting outside," I explained.

"Oh, I see."

"Well, Jesus, you don't have to sound so shocked. I may pick poorly, but men still do like me, believe it or not."

I grabbed a stray tarp, folded it, and stuck it behind the couch. I walked over to Mr. Spangler and looked him straight in the eye.

"I can't have you around. It'll freak me out just knowing you're here. I mean, even more than it does now."

"I understand."

"Good," I said, feeling empowered.

"Close your eyes, count to three, and I'll be gone."

I gave him an incredulous stare. "Really? That's what this has come to? Fine." I closed my eyes and counted to three.

I opened them again and Mr. Spangler was still standing in front of me with a big grin on his face.

"I do so enjoy my petty torments."

A knock came from the front door, followed by what sounded like a dog whimpering. I glanced over at the door.

"Shit. Please, you have to..."

I looked back and Mr. Spangler was gone.

"So we're clear?" There was no response. "Now just stay that way."

I walked over and let Finch in. He took stock of the apartment, which was still an unholy mess. "Man, this is pretty hardcore," he said, gazing at the maelstrom.

"It was much worse."

"I didn't know you were that much of an artist."

"Neither did I."

He walked around the living room, nodding his head in approval.

"When you said painting, I didn't know you meant *painting* painting. I thought you meant like redecorating."

"Hey, I like my drab earth tones," I said defensively.

"Show me something."

"Maybe later. C'mon, I'm hungry. Let's eat." I walked to the wine rack and pulled out a bottle. "Chili cheese fries goes with red, right?"

We sat on the balcony sharing a candlelit fast food dinner, serenaded by the occasional EMS siren or whir from a nearby police helicopter.

"I never would've figured you for a Southsider," said Finch.

"Actually, I grew up on the North Side, but I still don't really get that whole territorial thing."

"A lot of people will tell you it's all socioeconomics, but screw that. It's about baseball, pure and simple."

"Which I don't follow."

Finch stared at me in disbelief. "You could be excommunicated for that."

"Sorry," I said with no trace of remorse.

"I've always said, it's not Madison that divides the city, it's grown men playing a kid's game. To me, it's always been that simple."

"And which side do you fall on?"

"Neither. I'm a soccer fan."

He held a finger to his lips to let me know to keep his deep, dark confessional on the down-low.

"I'll take it to my grave," I promised.

Finch stared out at the scenery from my balcony, which consisted of an alley with utility poles, trash bins, and the back of other apartments.

"I like your view."

"Ha ha. Say what you want, but I got a great deal on this place."

"No, I'm serious. Imagine how dull it'd be if you just had a typical picturesque skyline. This way you're privy to all kinds of interesting shit that can go down."

"Like the stabbing across the way last week?"

"Well, there ya go! A cornucopia of life right before your eyes."

I poured myself some more wine and offered a refill to Finch, who declined.

"I'm good. If I get too drunk you'll try and take advantage of me."

"Lightweight."

He finished off his basket of fries and wiped his hands. Finch then leaned on his side to look at me.

"Let me ask you something. Now, I'm not trying to get all philosophical on you, but do you ever get the feeling sometimes that you're going to do something great with your life? But you don't know what, and you don't know how, and you don't know what you'd do even if you got there, but you do know it's where you should be?"

"That's philosophical?"

"Just roll with it."

"The answer is no."

"Hmm. Had you pegged all wrong then, I guess."

"You said sometimes. For me, it's every day."

Finch smiled. "Same here. Bugs the shit out of you, doesn't it? Okay, if reality hadn't so rudely interrupted, what would you have liked to have done with your life?"

"Fuck, you make it sound like I'm eighty and in a nursing home."

"Fair enough. I'll rephrase. Master plan. What would you like to be doing?"

I know it sounded like a relatively innocuous question, but I was completely astonished by it. Not because he was getting personal so fast, but because in all the time I'd been dating, no guy had ever asked me that.

Not one.

"Probably be an artist. Go live in Europe. Total cliché, right?"

"So what? I'd love to go there and write. Do the whole boho thing like in the fifties."

He picked up his wine and finished it off.

"That's it. I've just decided. We'll quit our jobs tomorrow, sell everything we own, and move to Paris. Goals, right?"

He held up his glass in a toast.

"It's bad luck to toast with an empty glass," I noted.

"Is that an Irish thing?"

"I think it's pretty much an everywhere thing."

"I'll risk it."

I raised my glass and clinked with him. "Goals," I reaffirmed.

He put his glass down and got up from the chair with a stagger.

"Whoa. Now if you'll excuse me. I have to go find *la toilette*."

When I walked back inside a bit later, carrying the bags and bottles from our feast, I was greeted by the sound of snoring. Finch had fallen asleep on the couch. I got a blanket out of the hallway closet and draped it over him, smiling at the serene expression on his face. Naturally, I couldn't resist playing with some of the facial ring piercings on him.

I've still got a lot of little kid left in me. Shocking, huh?

In the morning, I was gently awakened by the shrieking alarm from the smoke detector. I immediately jumped out of bed and was greeted by a white haze hanging in the hallway.

As I ran into the kitchen, I found Finch battling fires on two fronts, one in a pan he was holding, the other coming from the oven. He saw me and tried to offer reassurance.

"Don't worry. I got this," he yelled.

"Got what?! You're going to torch the place!"

He finally managed to quell the flames and breathed a sigh of relief. "I wanted to surprise you."

"Success!"

We sat at the kitchen counter eating the breakfast that Finch had so selflessly made. At least what was left of it. He gnawed on a blackened strip of bacon, while I sparred with a waterlogged omelet that kept dribbling through my fork. Even though it was pretty much a disaster, I found the whole thing rather charming. Effort counts a lot in this world.

"Charcoal is really not that bad for you," said Finch, looking at his nuked bacon strip.

"Yes, if you've been poisoned," I needled.

"I felt so bad for crapping out on you like I did last night. That's twice now. They're coming for my Man Card, I just know it. I figured this was the least I could do in terms of repentance."

"I appreciate it, and actually this omelet isn't too bad."

"Really? Thanks," he smiled, content his efforts were not in vain.

As he turned his back to grab some orange juice, I quickly removed a large piece of eggshell from my mouth.

"Okay, so you have to explain the paintings," he said.

"Explain what?"

"I hope you don't mind, but I peeked at what you've done and here's what I don't get. Why are you taking a beginning drawing class when you can paint like this?"

I quickly tried to come up with a good rationale, rather than anything approaching the truth. "Because, duh, I'm trying to get laid."

Nailed it. With emphasis.

We spent the next half hour cleaning up from the mess. Who would've ever figured scrubbing pots and washing dishes could be romantic, but it sort of was.

After that, we went into the living room to look at my paintings, which even I hadn't really taken full stock of yet. They all had that surrealistic bent that I loved, and actually, I was quite pleased.

"The first thing I want to know is what you took before you did these, and do you have any of it left?"

"I'm my own narcotic," I said drolly.

"These are really trippy."

"Is that good or bad?"

"Definitely good."

He pointed at one of the paintings, an airport tarmac with a plane ascending into a giant cobweb that'd been weaved across the sky.

"But this one is my favorite. What do you call it?"

"I don't have a name for it."

"C'mon, a painting has to have a name."

"You're the writer. You name it."

Finch picked up the painting to stare at it closer. After a few moments of intense consideration, he arrived at his answer.

"*Taking Off.*"

"Awfully generic, isn't it?"

He thought momentarily, then nodded. "You're right. "*Going Places.*" Does that work?"

"Yeah, that really saved it," I teased him.

"Can I have it?"

"I need it."

"For what?"

"I can't tell you. You'd run away."

Finch looked at me with imploring eyes.

"Sorry, I have to keep it," I held firm.

His expression changed to an exaggerated pout. "I'll give it a place of honor in my loft. I swear."

"No can do."

Sensing he wasn't getting anywhere, Finch hardened. This had come down to a battle of wills. "Either you give me the painting or I'll come over and cook again."

I caved. "Fine. Take it."

"Thanks!"

Seeming genuinely excited by his new acquisition, Finch held the painting out at arm's length to admire it again.

"Way cool," he said.

Nine

I was surprised at how well I'd settled into my new job and was even doing decent in terms of sales. I heard through office chatter that I possibly had the inside track on "Associate of the Month," an honor that I knew if I won, I would cherish forever.

I teared up just thinking about it.

You got your name on a plaque, although I was hoping for a little hardware too, like maybe a golden plunger or something like that.

I was at my desk cold-calling when my boss, Tate Henderson, or Hendu, as he liked everyone to call him, came up to my cubicle. He was an African-American in his late fifties, rotund and jovial, with a great laugh. You had a problem in life? Take it to Hendu. He'd help you figure it out by the end of the day. He was the only boss I'd ever had who was universally loved by all the employees, and was a main part of why I didn't hate the job like so many of my past grinds.

Somehow, he made selling ass gaskets tolerable.

"Hi, Emma, can I see you in my office for a minute?"

Was this about the award? Should I have prepared an acceptance speech? Do I tell him I consider it an honor just to be even nominated among the other employees? I was dizzy with anticipation.

I followed him into his office, which was decorated with various janitorial supply prototypes.

"Close the door and have a seat."

I shut the door and sat down across the desk from him. I was trying to get a read on things but came up empty.

He picked up a clipboard, flipped through some pages, then tossed the clipboard back on the desk. A troubled look crossed his face.

Uh oh. I'd seen expressions like that before. They were usually followed by, "Get the fuck out." Had I been totally wrong about this whole thing?

"Emma, how long have you been with us?"

"About two months."

"Do you like it here? I mean, do you get along with the other employees?"

It suddenly struck me what this whole thing could've been about. Why didn't I think of it earlier?

"Mr. Henderson, if this..."

"Hendu, please."

"Hendu, if this is about the microwave blowing up, I didn't..."

"The reason I ask is because you might not want to form too many close friendships."

My stomach sunk to my knees. Here we go again. I slumped slightly and looked down. I'd seen this movie before and it fucking sucked. Big time.

"And the reason I say that is because I think you're going to be a lot more valuable for us out in the field."

I looked up to see Hendu with a big smile on his face.

"I'm sorry, I don't understand," I said.

He held up the clipboard. "Your sales numbers are great."

"Oh. Okay, thanks," I said, totally relieved.

"Personally, I've always felt it's better to attach a face to the product, so we'd like you out there working as a sales rep to the merchants."

"I'm sorry, I'm not following. Isn't that what I do now?"

"Yes, but you'll be driving around and getting the A & J name out there. Now, the pay's the same, but you do get a gas allowance. The only thing you won't get is to see my handsome mug as much anymore. Real crusher, right?"

He handed me some brochures.

"Read up on these new urinal cakes and bowl brushes we're introducing next week, and you'll be right on top of things."

"Thanks," I said, forcing a weak smile as I took the info.

While new avenues to my employment had opened up, I have to admit I'd been slacking off when it came to finishing the paintings. I knew I wanted my privacy back, but at the same time, I was getting used to having Mr. Spangler around. Like the loopy relative that'd show up on holiday get-togethers. They'd embarrass themselves, but at the end of the night still slip you $50 on the way out just for being family.

In a strange way, he also motivated me to keep pecking away at exercising my creative muscles, which had totally atrophied over the years.

This, I imagine, was his intention all along.

I knew it was never going to lead anywhere, and once he left for good I'd probably resort to my usual unproductive ways, but it did keep me from feeling like such a worthless slug while I was at it.

And my relationship with Finch had started to get a little more serious. He took me on our first "official" date, which started in Wrigleyville, where I destroyed his ass on Pop-A-Shot. We then proceeded to hit up lots of funky bookstores and ended the night in a heated game of bar trivia, where the final tie-breaker question was to name the official language of the U.S. After a brief debate with Finch, I answered for us with "None." It then devolved into a shouting match with some drunken guy who kept screaming "English!!" with heavy emphasis on the first vowel.

Of course, I was right, but some people just had a hard time admitting defeat and before it came to blows, the host slapped a gift card in my hand and we bounced.

All in all, it made for a very memorable outing, but two things had yet to happen.

I'd not been to Finch's place yet, and we hadn't had sex. I was beginning to wonder if the two weren't somehow related. Was he actually married? Had a live-in lover? Ran an escort service?

I was itching to get this resolved, because I was starting to feel something deeper rather than just having a good time.

I think Finch was too.

Finally, he invited me over to his place in Ravenswood, a neighborhood that was this melting pot of an arts community, mixed in with industrial businesses and some distilleries thrown in for good measure. His loft was an old machine shop during the Depression that had been converted, and as I rode the freight elevator to his floor, I was just praying the belts holding that rickety crate up weren't from that era as well.

He and his roommates were having a party and he desperately wanted me to come. He said the reason I hadn't been asked over before was because the place was being redesigned, but now it was finally done. I let him know I was giving up a night of binge-watching *Peaky*

Blinders for this, so it'd damn well better be worth it.

I decided to wear my Moschino LBD, the one I gave thought to being buried in, and was understated as usual with my makeup and perfume. I had always been a minimalist when it came to slathering on the war paint, mostly because I was so fair-skinned I looked like fucking Pennywise when I put color on me.

As I walked into the loft, I saw Finch talking to a group of people. Upon seeing me, he immediately excused himself, came over, and gave me a big hug and kiss.

"You made it. Did you have any trouble finding the unit?"

"No, I just followed the trail of vomit from the elevator."

"Yeah, one of my roomie's friends had a little too much and staggered out of here."

As I looked around, I could see there was no rhyme or reason to the design of the loft. The furniture, fixtures, and rugs mixed art nouveau, French country, and Victorian into one heady mix, but somehow it all worked.

"So, this is the bus terminal." I nodded.

"Sorry it took so long to get you over here. Yep, the place reflects all of our tastes."

"You weren't kidding about the privacy though. Where's your corner of the world?"

Finch pointed over to a sliding French door partition in the back.

"That's my cubby hole. You want something to drink?"

"I just want to collapse. I've been on my feet all day."

"Doing what?"

"Well, let's see. Today I was out closing a deal for a fleet of multi-roll toilet paper dispensers. Very exciting stuff. You should blog about it."

"The dark underbelly of the janitorial supply world. I love it."

My attention caught on something very familiar on the wall near the entrance. It was the painting I had given to Finch. "Hey, I know who made that," I said, pointing at it.

"See, I told you. First thing you notice when you walk in."

"I'm honored. That's really sweet, thanks." I kissed him on the cheek.

I followed Finch across the loft, and we sat down on one of the most comfortable couches I had ever been on. I mean, I literally melted into it.

"Oh my God, I am never getting up from this couch," I declared.

"Tony scored this old Chesterfield for like $700 and we all fight each other to kick back on it."

"Who's Tony?"

"Oh, okay, let me give you the roomie lineup."

Finch pointed over to a heavyset guy wearing a Blackhawks jersey who was trying to do match tricks to impress a couple of girls, and not succeeding.

"That's Tony. He's an actuary. Terrible with women but has a heart of gold."

He then motioned toward an intense-looking man embroiled in a heated conversation.

"And that's Craig, he does web design, but don't talk to him."

"Why not?

"Because he'll just try and engage you in debates about existentialism, neoconservatism, and why the White Sox suck."

Finch nodded toward a tall, slender man with an indefatigable energy who was busy being the center of attention.

"And that's Darryl. He just got appointed artistic director at his dance company."

"Pretty diverse lineup."

"I guess. We try not to kill each other."

As the party wore on and we circulated among the crowd, I found myself totally digging the energy of the place.

I eventually wound up over at a portable bar by the entrance to make myself a drink. As I did so, I noticed a woman in her late thirties standing off to the side who just kept staring at my painting. She looked mildly eccentric to say the least, wearing a bright floral Haori jacket and giant oversized glasses that threatened to swallow her face.

She seemed almost transfixed by the painting.

"My God, what I wouldn't give for a Molly cap right now," she said to no one in particular.

"Sorry, fresh out," I responded.

"Hmm. Pity. There's nothing better than enhanced appreciation."

I looked under the bar and pulled out a bottle of tequila, holding it up as an offer in compromise.

"Got some Tequila Gold," I said as I glanced at the label. "Making people unconscious for ten generations."

The woman dismissed my offering. "Too pedestrian."

"Suit yourself," I shrugged and put the bottle back.

She returned to admiring the painting. "God, I really love the aesthetic of this."

"Thanks."

She looked at me with a mildly surprised expression.

"This is yours?"

"Guilty as charged," I said, raising my hand.

"Very impressive. And praise is something Berri doesn't give lightly. The luminosity is what's most striking. What did you use to achieve it?"

"I mixed the acrylics with a glaze modifier."

"Nice. Most artists blatantly overuse mediums. It's a sin. Did you underpaint first?"

"Nope."

"Interesting. What's your name and have I seen your work before?"

"Emma Connolly, and I guarantee you haven't."

"How long have you been at this?"

"You mean painting? Well, that's open to interpretation."

"How so?"

"I started very young and then...I'm kind of on and off."

The woman nodded and then looked at the cheese tray. I mean, *really* looked at the cheese tray. Like she was trying to pick out a perfect diamond. She finally settled on a cube, took a nibble out of it, and then slipped it into the pocket of her jacket.

"What brings you here?" she asked.

"Finch invited me."

"Ah, Finch. Amusing sort. I find his blogs mildly engaging. Displays an elevated wit mixed with an outsider's sentiment. Are you two dating?"

I had absolutely no idea what to make of this strange woman, who had gone back to scrutinizing the cheese again.

"Apropos of nothing. Let's just say we're enjoying each other's company."

"For how long?"

"Wow, you ask a lot of questions."

"Knowledge is power."

"Yes, and power corrupts," I said.

This caused the woman's face to light up as she looked at me with a Cheshire cat grin. "I know. Isn't it exquisite?"

She picked another cube off the tray and went through the same nibble-and-stash routine. Peculiar didn't even begin to cover it.

"We've been going out for a couple of months," I offered up.

"New love. When it's still fresh and vital. Before the casualty of corrosion takes its toll. Berri envies you."

She gestured to the painting. "Do you have any more like this?"

"A few."

She took out a business card and handed it to me.

"Well, anytime you have something you want to show me, do give me a call. I'm always looking to buy good art. And this is good art. Keep doing what you're doing."

She walked away to join the rest of the party, while I looked at the card. Finch came over to grab a beer out of the cooler.

"That was random," I said.

"What was?"

"This woman I was just talking to. I didn't know whether to tell her to fuck off or make her my bestie."

"Who?"

I showed him the business card.

"Berri. That's Craig's boss. What did she say?"

"She kept referring to herself in third person, which always freaks me out."

"Illeism."

"What?"

"It's called illeism."

"Okay, well, it's just bizarre. Anyway, she said she really liked my painting, oh, and that we're doomed. She was also looking for drugs, which is not surprising."

"Yeah, she's definitely out there."

"And she said that your column was 'mildly engaging.'"

"Blog, not column. Columnists answer to corporate overlords, we don't."

"Sorry, didn't know it was such a sensitive issue."

"I'm kidding, although columnists probably get full medical, though. Bastards."

I glanced back down at the card.

"Sounds like you have a fan," Finch added.

I shrugged and pocketed the card, not thinking much of the odd encounter.

Some people just have an incredible talent for self-promotion. For broods like the Kardashians or the *Real Housewives of the Nine Circles of Hell,* it's their life blood. For me, though, I'd always chosen to blend into the background. Of course, when you really got to know me it was hard to get me to shut up, but as far as blowing my own horn, I hated the concept.

Maybe that's why I found it so mystifying that I arrived at the decision I did.

I was having lunch at my favorite Asian fusion restaurant, and as I slurped down a big bowl of chicken udon, I sat and stared at Berri's business card. She had no last name, which was somewhat fitting. Why settle for anything else? During our conversation, she'd said something that had just stuck with me. When she mentioned that she bought art, a primal instinct buried somewhere deep inside clicked on.

What if I could monetize my paintings? I know, it brought out the capitalist in me, but I was barely scraping by with this new job, and the chance to maybe make a few extra bucks could be like oxygen for me. It gets really, really old always being in survival mode.

I took the initiative and called her. I got put on hold forever, which made me almost want to hang up. I have a low threshold for "ignore" when it comes to calls, brought on by my years in phone sales. Many a customer service rep felt my wrath when they hung me out to dry while they checked with supervisors, or some other worthless excuse because they didn't know how to do their J.O.B.

Patience was not a virtue. It was a waste of my fucking time.

When Berri finally came on, I suddenly got nervous.

Insert the definition of irony here. Yes, I sold over the phone for a living, but that was for someone else. When it came to selling myself, it was much more personalized. Much more intimate. I was now trying to impose my will regarding me.

Not urinal cakes. Not tampon machines. *Me.*

Still, I had come this far and knew I had to press on.

"Hello," she said in that oddly inflected voice of hers.

"Hi, this is Emma Connolly. I met you at a party a couple of weeks ago."

"Which one, darling? I go to many."

"The one at Finch's place. I'm the girl with the painting you liked."

God, that was weak. Like I was groveling for approval or something. After a few moments of silence, she finally responded with what sounded like a cooing sound.

"Ooh, yes. How are you, dear?"

"I'm fine. I just wanted to say it was a pleasure meeting you. You're a fascinating person."

"Yes, Berri gets that a lot," she laughed.

"I was just following up on your offer. You said you'd be interested in any other art I may have."

Somewhere inside my brain, my id, ego, and super-ego were having a barroom brawl. I was basically trying to sell myself as an artist.

Which I wasn't.

"Oh, yes."

"Well, if possible, I'd like to show you some additional work I've done."

"But of course. Talk to my assistant and we'll schedule a time for you to come in."

"That's great. Thanks so much."

"I'll get her back on the line. Lovely to talk to you."

Short, sweet, and to the point. Just how I liked it. I exhaled. I also got put back on hold, and although it took the assistant forfuckingever to come back on, this time I didn't care.

A little window had been opened, and now I wanted to crawl right through it.

I took the next week and a half to finish two more paintings, and then I was faced with a huge problem. Which ones should I take to show her?

There were only six to begin with, well, five since Finch had one, but I was unsure which would get the best response.

I sat on the floor of the living room looking over the choices. Mr. Spangler was on the couch and I could tell he was getting frustrated with my self-manufactured dilemma.

"I don't know. Which do you think are the best?" I asked.

"It's art. There is no 'best.'"

"Not helping," I said. "I don't want to bring too many because that'll make me look thirsty, but if I don't bring enough it'll look like a hobby."

"Are you always this indecisive?" asked Mr. Spangler.

"It depends."

I took another look at the paintings and finally made the choice.

"Okay, these three then."

I picked up the canvasses, slipped them inside a large valise, and zipped them up. I stood and took a deep breath.

"So, wish me luck," I said to Mr. Spangler.

"No."

"Or not."

"Luck is what amateurs rely on. I wish you success."

I smiled. "I like that."

I paused for a moment, then unzipped the valise. "I don't know. Did I choose the right ones?"

All Mr. Spangler could do was roll his eyes, and I can't say I really blamed him.

Berri's office was on the Magnificent Mile, a section of town I'd always had a love/hate relationship with. If you could ignore the inherently touristy nature of the area, it had some great coffee shops and watering holes, as well as always being a favorite stretch for protest activity. I had joined Aaron there to march when the hotel workers went on strike. I remember thinking that I would've made a great anarchist had I been alive in the sixties, although I probably would've gotten bored with all the meetings and lack of fashion sense.

I took the elevator up to Berri's office on what seemed liked the 599th floor of a glass and steel monolith that scarred the skyline. Actually, I took it up three times, as I was early and the elevator was one of those really fast ones where it felt like you got that mini g-force thing going. Luckily, I had two express trips, but on the third one, some suits got on at the 32nd floor and I gave them an appropriate dirty look for fucking up my ride. I take thrills where I can get them.

I waited in a cavernous lobby, seated in front of this monstrous piece of architecture that looked like it was ready to fall off the wall at any given moment and squash me. I thought I'd be all fidgety, yet surprisingly, I was pretty relaxed. I wasn't expecting shit out of this, but at least it gave me a purpose, a feeling I'd lacked for some time.

Berri's assistant, a perfectly perfect girl named Elodie, came out to greet me. She was flawless in almost every way imaginable, with the possible exception of not having a personality, a sense of humor, or an ounce of warmth. Minor quibbles that I gladly would've traded to look like that. Why she was working as an assistant, I had no idea. She was a James Bond villainess come to life who should've been out seeking world domination instead.

"Emmy, I'm Elodie."

"Hi. It's Emma."

"Excuse me?"

"Emma, with an 'a.'"

She didn't acknowledge my correction as she turned and motioned for me to follow her.

"Please come with me."

I picked up my valise and followed her down a long corridor. The walls and hallway were decorated with impressive pieces of abstract art and sculpture, meaning if this was the office standard, I would be done in about two minutes with my feeble efforts.

"What do you guys do here?"

"Software development," she said in a voice so flat, I wanted to recommend Auto-Tune for her.

"Great. Can you help me fix my laptop?" I joked.

Elodie offered no response, and we just kept walking.

"It keeps crashing on me," I followed up, hoping to spark some human interaction. Absolutely nothing. Just the tap-tap-tap from her black satin Louboutins.

Okay, so small talk was off the table. Might as well play this out.

"Must be all those bondage videos I'm downloading, huh? Just can't get enough."

Nope. Obviously she wasn't a fan of the fine arts.

She stopped walking and pointed at the door.

"That's Berri's office. She's waiting for you. Can I get you some water?"

"No, I'm..."

Without missing a beat, Elodie turned and walked away before I could finish my sentence.

"...good," I said.

My paintings rested on easels in Berri's office, which was a scaled-down version of what I'd just passed in the hallway, crammed with art, rugs, and books. Hardly what you'd expect to find in a software development company.

She sat and contemplated the paintings with a meditative look on her face. I was seated across from her, having a staring contest with a huge 200-pound English Mastiff that was hunkered down beside her.

And losing.

Fucking dog never blinked. It was as big as me and could have devoured me in one bite. As if that wasn't unsettling enough, next to the dog was a large hookah pipe, which it took a hit off and then returned to staring at me.

Swear. To. God.

"Well, well, well," said Berri as she got up from her chair. She approached each painting closer, turned to me as if to say something, then went back to studying the pieces.

"And you've had no formal training?" she said.

"Not really. I'm pretty much self-taught."

"How rich," she purred.

"Am I? Oh, not at all," I said, not realizing it wasn't a question. Genius, Em.

"No, I mean that you haven't had any formal training. That's what makes these even better. They're raw and unfettered."

She sat back down, turned to her dog and French kissed him, then returned her attention to me.

"Understand that I work in a world of codes, modules, and procedures. Everything specific and precise. Very boring stuff. That's why Berri likes her art to be the exact opposite. An explosion of the mind, if you will. These show a wonderfully propulsive, chaotic ambience."

"Thanks," I said, hoping she'd translate. I think it was a compliment.

"What else are you working on?"

Uh oh, it sounded like the start of an exit line.

"Various things. I'm always keeping busy." What, gaming and smoking out don't count as staying busy?

"Well, I hope Berri doesn't insult you."

"Why would you do that?" I laughed nervously.

"Because I only want one of these. At least for now."

"No, it generally takes a lot more for me to be insulted."

Berri pointed at one of the paintings. She'd chosen the one I'd done of a grove filled with burning trees, with plumes of black smoke turning into symbols from the periodic elements chart.

"What's this one called?"

"*Poplar Science.*"

Berri smiled and nodded. "Clever."

I'd taken Finch's advice and decided to name everything. I wasn't trying to make some climate change statement with it, I was just trying to be a smartass and come up with a funny quip. Guess it worked, but for me, coming up with names was harder than painting.

"Did you have a price in mind for it?"

"Not really, no," I replied.

I watched as Berri took out a ledger. She scribbled out a check, signed her name with a flourish, and handed it to me.

"How's that for insulting?"

I glanced at the check. It was for $500.

I immediately went all tingly inside. Like the time I won $100 on a Glittering Gems scratcher.

"I think I'll live. Thank you," I tossed off with all the cool of someone holding pocket aces.

"I'm glad you decided to call me. A lot of artists are horrible at the pursuit. Just creating does not suffice. Follow-up is everything in life. Do give me your contact information."

"Here, I have a card," I said as I dug into my purse. I pulled out an A & J Janitorial Supplies business card, complete with my name and a drawing of a big red plunger on it.

Oh hell no! I quickly put it back.

"Nope, wrong card. I'll just write down my info."

I jotted it on a piece of scratch paper and handed it to Berri.

"A worthy piece of advice. If you're serious about doing this on a larger scale, you need to start traveling in the right circles. The world is littered with the carcasses of artists who are cult failures. If you're interested, there's a little soiree I'd like to invite you to next weekend."

Are you fucking kidding? Social invitations had been so few and far between over the past year, I practically qualified as a shut-in.

"Sure, sounds great. Thanks."

I walked out of Berri's office on air, then dashed to the restroom, the valise banging against my leg. I called Finch to give him the news. I tend to squeak when excited, so I probably sounded like I was on helium.

"Hey, it's me. You're not going to believe what happened."

"You got arrested?" said Finch.

"No."

"You got in an accident?"

"No. Jesus, why would you say that?"

"I default to worst case scenarios."

"No, I just got through seeing Berri."

"Wait, that was today?"

I let out an exasperated groan. "Yes, it was today!"

"So what happened?"

"She bought one of my paintings."

"No way! For how much?"

"$500!" I squealed.

"That's great! Let's go to Vegas and spend it on strippers and blow."

I looked at my phone. Do I hang up now and be done with it?

"I'm joking, I'm joking. Em, that's wonderful. Congrats, I'm so stoked for you. We have to celebrate. Hey, I'm late for a meeting, but call me later and we'll figure it out."

"Okay, bye."

I hung up, still electrified from what had just happened.

On my way out, I ran into Elodie, who gave me a real Elsa smile. Frozen as fuck.

"How did it go?" she asked.

I just looked at her with a wicked smirk and walked away.

Ten

Knowing my affinity for retro, Finch had me meet him to celebrate at The McKlintock over in Wicker Park. It was another of those old places that had started life as an office building in the twenties, sat vacant and lonely for years, but had now been converted into this sublime deco hotel with gorgeous views of the city skyline. He snagged a cabana on the rooftop, ordered up a bottle of Dom, and we spent the evening drinking and lounging on the most wonderful of spring nights. I had half a mind to strip down and jump into the infinity pool that stretched out before us, although I'm guessing the staff might've frowned upon such behavior.

We made it a point not to get too buzzed like some of our previous outings together because we wanted to savor this. When it got to be around midnight, Finch looked at me and asked, "Do you want to go?"

"No way," I strongly declined. The night was too fucking magical to end so soon, and yes, midnight is way too early. Practically middle of the day in my book.

"So, do you want to stay?"

"Pretty much covers the bases," I laughed.

"No, I mean do you want to *stay*."

Finch flashed his best bad boy grin. And with that it was on. Big time.

We sprinted down to the front desk to check on vacancies. We would've taken a broom closet with an inflatable chair. It didn't matter. Even though it was the weekend, there were a few rooms available. Without even bothering to ask about amenities, we grabbed one. It turned out neither one of us had gone to our senior proms, so here we were acting like a couple of giddy high schoolers trying to make up for lost time.

When we got up to the room, it was definitely on the smaller and somewhat spartan side, but that just added to the appeal. It had a total Euro vibe. Clothes came off in record time, but before we settled in for the evening's main event, we spent about twenty minutes just slow-dancing naked in front of a window to music we cobbled together from Finch's phone playlist. We debated a little over what bops to include, but finally reached an agreement. It's a real art when it comes to deciding whether to grind to Queen Bey, Lana Del Rey, or John Legend, however, I did draw the line at including Ed Sheeran, and I'm Irish.

Since there weren't any buildings across the way, no one could see us and even if someone could, I didn't care. Not that I was some brazen exhibitionist, but this was just sensual, sexy fun, helped by the fact Finch's body smelled like sandalwood, my favorite scent. And to answer a question I raised a while back, no, he wasn't sporting the Prince Albert look which didn't bother me one way or the other. I just wanted him to be good.

Before my relationship with Aaron, who was mundane at best, a lot of my sexploits would've qualified as downright poor to freakish. I dated a guy named Josh for about two months, but finally had to break it off because his idea of great sex was having me yank on him while he kept whispering in my ear, "Are you ready to accept it?"

Seriously.

I was more worried about my health, not because he had some disgusting STD, but because I was always close to bursting a blood vessel to keep from laughing whenever he started that moronic mantra.

Then there was Arturo, a triathlete I dubbed Slap Happy, who I met while working at the tanning salon. He looked like he was chiseled by Rodin, but that sure as hell didn't do it for me. I gave him that nickname because he always wanted me to slap myself on the cheeks with his mutantly oversized member. I guess it was some power trip for him, or maybe a result of all the creatine he took, but it lasted for about three weeks and then I ghosted him. Normally, I think that's a pretty crappy thing to do to someone, but my self-preservation (and facial structure) depended on it.

I had even less than spectacular results in my one and only experience with a girl during my brief heteroflexible, bi-curious phase. Her name was Dani, and when I was at the Arts Institute I hung around with her from time to time. She was an animation major and I knew she liked me, but I was always a bit reticent. One rainy, miserable winter night, however, enough vodka finally broke down those walls and we went back to her place. She had this amazingly flawless skin and these really long, elegant fingers. Little did I realize those alluring digits would nearly turn out to be lethal weapons, as she proceeded to fingerblast me and basically scrape an inch off my cervix with her craggy-ass nails.

After about fifteen minutes where I thought my uterus was going to fall out, I finally mentioned that it kind of hurt. I thought for sure my continual wincing would've been a solid hint. She profusely apologized and got out a pair of clippers to trim down her talons. How sweet and considerate, I thought, that is until she decided to go full day spa on me, spending the next half hour filing her nails after cutting them.

I was surprised she didn't go for a base coat and French tips next considering the whole mood had been completely and utterly killed. We wound up talking about nail polish after that, and never did get back to the matter at hand. Pun intended.

I could go on, but why belabor the issue? Everyone has had bad sex. Sucks at the time, but makes for great stories later on. Ultimately, I loved the warm cocoon of a committed relationship, but there was also something to be said for a well-placed dalliance here and there.

Which leads me back to my first night with Finch, well, in the biblical sense. He couldn't have been more affectionate and attentive, as he spent way more than the Minimum Daily Requirement on foreplay, although I think he got a little bothered that I kept twisting his nipple ring like I was starting a Volvo. I liked to keep things fun in bed, mainly because it put everything on an even keel. I wasn't exactly a wallflower harboring a secret desire to be dominated, although we did agree our safe word would be "Republican," because honestly, who wants to keep fucking after hearing that?

For the next five hours we went at it like Walmart shoppers on Black Friday. I won on the orgasm scoreboard 4–3, but Finch was cool with that. No wounded male ego problems there. We also worked in lots of time for cuddling and playing with Alexa, as Finch peppered her with rude questions about her sex life and if she'd ever consider a threesome with Siri.

Everything was perfect with one small exception. It was during the third go-round, I think, when right in the middle of mid-thrust, Finch stopped. Stone cold dead. Like he realized he forgot to turn the stove off while on vacation. He pulled out bareback, the condom having come off.

Vanished. Poof.

It was nowhere to be found, and we looked everywhere. I even excused myself to go to the bathroom for a little self-exploratory adventure but came up empty. Eventually he rewrapped, and we went on with the show.

It wound up being a wickedly good night and we spent the rest of the weekend together. I know most relationships start off with a lot of fire and passion before they can dissolve into boredom, familiarity, or even contempt. What was it Berri said, "The casualty of corrosion," but I had a good feeling about this, and optimism was something I dealt out with stunning irregularity.

By the way, the missing condom was eventually located, found by my gynecologist a few days later. During a routine exam, I mentioned what had happened and with speculum in hand, she went on a search party and found it tucked away in an upper canal corner. I was too embarrassed to tell Finch of the discovery for fear he'd think some vaginal dentata possibly awaited him next.

Believe it or not, I didn't deposit Berri's check for three days. It sat on my living room mantel, where I could look at it whenever I walked in. No one had paid me for anything I had ever made, so I wanted to savor it, like those businesses that framed their first dollar ever earned.

The closest I'd come to a creative-based financial transaction was when I was eleven and made a dreamcatcher for Cathy Gromacki, my next-door neighbor, in exchange for a Britney CD. I spent two days working on it and thought it was beautiful. I really wanted to keep it for myself, but a deal was a deal, so I gave it to Cathy. What I got back was a used CD with a cracked jewel case, torn insert, and skipped all over the place. I was furious and confronted her about it. She argued that she never promised me a new one, and I guess technically she was right. It did put a rift in our friendship, though, and when she finally moved, I remember standing outside giving her the finger as she and her parents drove away.

Sometimes I'm just so sentimental.

Bills were coming due, so down came the check from the mantel, but that didn't mean I was any less geeked about the whole episode. I stared at it as I walked to the counter to put it in my purse.

"You look baffled."

I spun around, giving Mr. Spangler a dirty look for startling the shit out of me *yet again*. He was leaning against the bookcase with his arms crossed.

"About what?" I said.

He nodded toward the check. "About that."

I held up the check. "This? This feels all kinds of freaky."

"Why? Because someone recognized your talents?"

"No, because it means I can finally pay my rent on time," I reasoned. "Well, what you said too."

I stuffed it in my purse and turned to look at Mr. Spangler. "Hey, I just thought of something. I'm not going to have to do extra paintings because I sold one and gave another one away, am I?"

Mr. Spangler just smiled at me.

"Well?" I pressed.

He said nothing and just continued to smile.

"Please stop with that blissed-out grin. It so creeps me out," I said.

"Our agreement is complete."

"But I've only done six paintings. The agreement was eight, I thought."

"That was before extenuating circumstances. The fact that you've now started a career makes the rest of agreement null and void."

"Don't bullshit me. I'll lawyer up on you," I threatened.

He walked over to the living room table, looking quite pleased with himself. "I'll be leaving you on your own, Miss Connolly, but I do hope you'll continue down the creative path. Promise me that you won't abandon it?"

"Are you kidding? You think I want to sell plungers and toilet bowl cleaners the rest of my life?"

"That's not a promise, that's an evasion," he stated.

"Yes, I promise."

"Then my time here has been well spent."

"So that's it? You're just going to walk in the closet and leave?"

"Something like that. I may be gone, but in my place there'll be someone else."

I gave him a distrustful stare. "Who?"

"'Emma Connolly, professional artist.'"

I laughed out of force of bad habit. "Hardly, but it sounds good."

"Everyone starts with a single sale. You're now officially tied with Van Gogh."

"Yeah, right. I'll call up MoMA and ask them when the hell's my retrospective."

My cell rang and I answered it. "Hello? No, I said it's on the second floor. That's not even our building. I know it looks the same, but... look, I'll be right out."

I hung up, completely aggravated. I glanced over at Mr. Spangler. "I'll be right back. I have to go rescue the delivery guy before he winds up in Lake Michigan."

I went outside to meet the driver. He was sweating profusely from having run the gauntlet of trying to find my apartment. I felt bad for him and tipped him extra, then spent a few minutes extensively detailing how he could get back out. Here's hoping that he's been heard from since.

When I came back to the apartment, Mr. Spangler was gone.

Again.

I called out, checked the living room closet, but not a trace. I know what he said about leaving, although I couldn't really be sure if this was for good. He did like to fuck with me that way.

As I sat eating dinner at the kitchen counter, it really started to bug me that I didn't get the chance to thank him. He was the change I didn't know I needed and I wanted to tell him so, but for whatever reason, he chose not to stick around.

I suddenly noticed something sitting on the living room table. I walked over to it and saw it was a small bag of weed with a note attached that read, "All right, so I took more than a little. P.S. - I'm lousy at goodbyes."

So that was it. No closure, no nothing. It was not acceptable.

Eleven

The party that Berri had invited me to was in Lake Forest, a wealthy enclave about forty minutes outside the city and three lifetimes away from anything I'd ever seen before. I gave my name at the gate (yes, it was that kind of place) and we drove up a driveway that was the size of your average alien crop circle. Finch and I gazed in amazement at the sheer size of the French Normandy house that sat majestically before us. As we got out of the car, a valet came over to take my keys. I felt embarrassed he was going to park my Mini amongst a Buggati, a Lamborghini, and a McLaren, just to name a few of the other vehicles that were already ostentatiously hogging the driveway.

"No joyriding in the car, please," I said to the valet.

The valet laughed and nodded. "I'll fight the urge."

As Finch and I walked towards the mansion, which was still a good fifty yards on, he slowly turned a 180 to take in the scope of the place.

"Should we just Uber the rest of the way?" Finch suggested.

"No shit."

"Whose place is this again?"

"I looked it up online and it said it's part of some really old Chicago money. Been passed down from generation to generation."

"And how do I get in on this?"

"Be reincarnated," I said.

As impressive as the place was outside, the inside was equally opulent. Fresco ceilings, giant Persian rugs, antiques, and white marble everywhere. The only thing missing was a guide to lead us on a tour of the palatial estate. The crowd was a well-dressed, monied bunch, lots of designer clothes, while I was rocking my Forever 21 cami dress and faux suede crisscross mules. Total cost for the outfit: $45. Take that, you fashionistas.

Servers breezed by with silver trays, trying to ply us with drinks and hors d'oeuvres, but both of us were too caught up in the surroundings to indulge just yet. I felt like an extra on the set of some wealth porn movie.

We walked out to the backyard, which opened into an area that made the Gardens of Versailles look impoverished. A four-piece string quartet played Coldplay songs on the main landing, while a sprawling lawn led to a sunken tennis court, geometrically shaped topiaries, and a large grotto. The place was the most blatant example of conspicuous consumption I'd ever seen.

And I loved every minute of it.

I grew up lower-middle class, but one thing my dad had said that always stuck with me was never envy, envision instead. Obviously, I couldn't imagine a life like this but I knew what he meant. Finch and I stood there soaking it up, unsure what to do next.

"What time do you think Gatsby rolls in?" Finch asked.

"No idea, but this is definitely not my crowd."

"Well, you need to make them your crowd so when you become successful, I can be the leeching boyfriend."

"Boyfriend?" I said with an arched eyebrow.

"Okay, leeching hanger-on."

We migrated over to a massive food table that was adorned with giant ice sculptures. As we scanned the offerings, a diminutive man in his thirties waddled up to us and looked at me.

"I hear you're someone I should know," he said.

"Me?"

"Yes."

I was surprised at his brash assumption. "Who said that?"

"Berri."

"Oh, where is she? Is she here yet? I have to thank her for inviting us."

"She's somewhere among the throng. Watching and processing," he said.

"Is this her house?" I asked.

"Oh lord, no. It's too flamboyant, even for her. By the way, I'm Tomas Winston. I write for the contemporary art section of the *Sentinel*."

"Emma Connolly."

We shook hands. Yeeesh. He had one of those clammy, skin-crawling, sweaty-palm handshakes. The kind that'd take half a bottle of Purell just to rid yourself of the gooey residue. I discreetly wiped my hand off on the back of Finch's jacket as I introduced him.

"This is Finch."

"Nice to meet you," said Tomas to Finch, who slightly grimaced upon receiving the hyperhidrosis special from Tomas.

Finch subtly tried to return the favor by wiping his hand on the back of my dress, but I deftly deflected it away.

"Can I ask you something? As a newspaper columnist, do you guys get full medical coverage?" Finch asked.

"Of course," Tomas confirmed.

"Fuck! I knew it."

"So, what exactly did she say about me?" I said, steering the conversation away before it got contentious.

"That your work is compelling and well worth seeking out."

I laughed and shook my head. "I don't know about that, but that's awfully nice of her to say."

"You'll have to excuse Emma. She's defectively modest," Finch said to Tomas.

"We do love to break stories on emerging artists. There's nothing more exciting than fresh blood in the talent pool. Do you have a website?"

"Uh, no," I said quietly, sorely realizing how many millions of miles away I was from even being remotely considered real.

"Well, if you have an exhibition, I'd love to come see it."

"I hadn't planned on it, but sure," I said.

At this point I probably came across like someone who sold velvet clown paintings at flea markets.

He handed me a business card. "This has both my home and work numbers on it."

"Great. Thanks," I said.

"Nice to meet you." He held eye contact for just that extra beat, then walked back into the crowd.

Finch shook his head. "I don't know, I just get the worst feeling I'm going to have to wind up fighting him for you."

"Will you stop?" I grabbed Finch by the sleeve and pulled him back over to the food table. He tried another run at wiping his hand on me, but I was having none of it and smacked it away again.

My culinary tastes have always run pretty simple, so it's no wonder I hadn't a clue what most of the offerings spread out before us were. Naturally, I did what anyone with great inquisitiveness would do; I started pointing at stuff. The scientific method always works best.

"Excuse me, what's that?" I asked the chef behind the table.

"Roasted pepper and anchovy crostini," he replied.

I pointed to a small bowl of...something. "And that?"

"Black olive tapenade."

"That one?"

"Smoked salmon blinis."

Rather than continue to harass the poor guy, I picked up one of the blinis and stuffed it in Finch's unsuspecting mouth.

"Well?" I queried Finch.

He chewed it around, then reluctantly swallowed. His expression told me it was a non-starter.

"Hmm. My official food taster says no," I said to the chef. "Do you have anything for the less discerning palate? We're unrefined."

We finally threw together a couple plates of food that looked edible, grabbed some wine, and staked out a corner of the landing.

"Can you imagine what the upkeep must be for this place?" Finch wondered.

"If you're living here, I don't think that's one of your worries," I reasoned.

"I guess. When I was a kid I used to take the Pace from Melrose Park to go into downtown, and I always remember going past some of those great houses in River Forest and just gawking at them. One of the regular bus drivers I had used to say it wasn't about the houses, it was about who was inside them. That's always stuck with me when I see places like this."

"What was there?"

"Where?"

"Downtown."

"Oh man, everything. Life, energy, and it wasn't the suburbs. But mainly I went for the library. I absolutely lived there on weekends. Ran up and down those floors filling my brain with random facts and trivia. It made me into the fount of useless information I am today."

I looked at Finch and smiled. "Well, not *so* useless."

As I continued to gaze over the crowd, I bit into a crepe and froze. I couldn't believe what I was seeing. Down below was Bolan, standing among the crowd and talking to a middle-aged couple.

"No way," I said.

"What?"

"What's he doing here?"

"Who??"

"My weed dealer."

Bolan's attention drifted up and caught on me. He did a double take, then broke into a big smile. Finch followed my stare and nodded toward Bolan.

"That guy's your dealer?" Finch said, more than a little surprised.

"Yep."

"No he's not. He's *The Bachelor*."

"Tell me about it."

Bolan excused himself from the people he was talking to and walked up the stairs toward us. He was accompanied by a shy-looking girl wearing a gorgeous teal green metallic dress. I was immediately impressed by her fashion taste.

"Fill me in. Did you guys used to date? Has he been to prison?" Finch asked.

"What? No. I was at the Arts Institute with him and then he made a fortune selling, but don't say anything unless he brings it up."

"That's why I asked. Always like to know the parameters."

It was hugs and handshakes all around as everyone introduced themselves. The first thing I noticed was Bolan had his swagga back. Whatever had been bothering him the last few times I'd seen him had seemingly been banished. I wasn't sure if it was because of the new girl he was with, but I was happy for him regardless.

He said he'd been invited by one of his upscale customers who wanted to help him expand his base. I told him how coincidental that was because I was there for the same reason, except for the whole pharmaceutical thing.

His date's name was Sheridan, which I thought was unusual. She said it meant "searcher" in Irish and that immediately put her in my good graces. She looked a couple years older than me and was definitely on the quiet side, content to alternate between gazing adoringly at Bolan and shooting me wary stares, although I had no idea why. Probably that territorial bullshit some women have about men, even when it's not remotely applicable like it was between Bolan and me. She was so not the type he used to go out with, who were usually all smokeshows that looked like they fell off the pages of *Maxim*. She did, however, have the most inhumanly beautiful crystal blue eyes I'd ever seen.

The interesting thing is how well Bolan and Finch got on, like some long-lost frat brothers. It was bromance at first sight.

I pried myself away from their male bonding long enough to hunt down a way to satisfy my daily sugar mania. Spread out at the end of the main food table was the most obscene assemblage of desserts I'd ever seen: tarts, truffles, brownies, lava cakes, all gathered in an unspeakable orgy of chocolate. I briefly gave thought to how fast I could run holding both trays.

"I know all about you," said a voice from behind me.

I turned around to find Sheridan staring at me with her arms at her side and both fists balled up. Well, this is interesting, because girlfriend looked like she was ready to throw down.

"You do?"

Sheridan nodded, then raised her fists slightly and opened her hands.

"Guarantee you these Green Hornets are better than anything on that table," she said with a devilish smile. Inside her hands was an assortment of gummy bears.

Aww, I thought. Here was someone after my own heart, but I knew if I started down that path, I'd be sloppy for the rest of the day.

"Thanks, but no."

She seemed genuinely surprised at my rejection of her offer. "Oh, okay."

"Don't worry, you didn't get any bad intel. It's just that I need to be sharp."

Wow, a major sea change must've been going on with me if I was rejecting free CBD edibles.

"Bolan says you used to paint," Sheridan said.

For some reason her comment struck a nerve with me and I don't know why. Maybe it was because it had this strange ring of finality to it, like a portion of my life was being officially declared dead. Even though it certainly didn't apply to things recently, I still bristled at the thought that someone would make such a pronouncement about me.

"I still do," I said.

"That's great, I've always wanted to learn."

"Take classes."

"Who's got the time, right? Besides, I'm way too old. You have to start that stuff when you're young," Sheridan said.

"No, you don't," I corrected her.

"Plus, I'm working two jobs," she tacked on to the avoidance list.

I didn't argue any further. There's no point in trying to convince someone of something when they've pulled up stakes on their life.

"You know, Bolan is a terrific sculptor," I said.

Sheridan looked surprised. "He is?"

"He's never mentioned it?"

"No. We pretty much talk about money, clothes, and furniture."

So that was the common ground! I was trying to figure out what the link was between her and Bolan. She seemed passive and resigned, while when operating at full speed, Bolan was the polar opposite. It was definitely an odd pairing, but if it worked, more power to 'em.

Blatant materialism can be such a beautiful bond.

"You really should encourage him to get back into it," I said, but my words just blew by Sheridan.

I glanced up on the balcony and saw Berri walking among the partygoers. Her outfit was what first caught my eye, an orange pantsuit infused with feathers on the sleeves and pant legs.

"Excuse me a sec, I have to go talk to someone," I said.

"Sure, no problem."

I took another quick glance at the dessert tray, grabbed an eclair off it, and started to head up the stairs toward Berri.

After a couple of steps, I stopped.

I don't know what possessed me, but I felt I just had to say something. I turned and walked back to Sheridan, who was digging into some German chocolate cake.

"Listen, when all those reasons you gave for not learning to paint become excuses, take classes. You won't regret it."

I smiled and left Sheridan looking a little shell-shocked that I'd even addressed the issue. As I went back up the stairs, I motioned to Finch where I was going. He waved, then returned to talking to Bolan.

I found Berri by the koi pond, staring intently at the fish swimming around in a massive kaleidoscope of color. These weren't your average aquarium kind, though, these were those monster three-footers who looked like they'd been spawned in Chernobyl.

"Berri, hi," I said.

"Did you know that koi will eat their young until they start to show color?"

"Sounds like horrific parenting skills."

She looked at me and grinned. "You're very sharp."

"I try," I said. Jesus, did I just sort of humble brag? Someone take me out to the woodshed. Now.

"How have you been, darling?"

"I'm great. I just wanted to thank you for inviting me here."

"Are you and Finch enjoying yourselves?"

"This place is unreal."

She took me by the arm and led me out of earshot from other people. "Oh good God, it's so garish. Every time I come here it reminds me of some Eurotrash fever dream. I always feel compelled to douche after I leave here."

"Probably wasn't going to be my first reaction, but okay."

"I see you met Tomas," she said, then leaned in closer to me. "I sicced him on you."

"We just talked briefly."

"Wonderful. Never share too much. Create a mystique, but he's a good person to have in your corner."

At this point in my life, I wasn't even aware I had a corner for anyone to occupy, but I wasn't going to question it.

We walked to the railing of the balcony as Berri noshed on appetizers.

I looked at what she was eating and nodded toward her plate. "What are those?" I said, continuing my exhaustive line of food questioning.

"Bacon-wrapped dates. They're so disgustingly delicious. Have one."

I picked one up and took a bite. "Oh fuck," I moaned in orgasmic delight.

"Is it not the greatest? Berri's made a complete pig of herself with these."

As I continued to relish my favorite new food, I looked out at the crowd below. "Who are these people?"

"A lot of them are involved in the arts scene, plus the usual contingent of wannabes. Talent will always attract them. Like moths immolating themselves in flame," Berri said with a dramatic flair.

"You have the most interesting way of speaking."

She lowered her sunglasses and peered at me. "Yes, and it scares the living shit out of most people."

We returned to people-watching when Berri suddenly let out a small cry of surprise as she looked out over the crowd.

"What?" I asked.

She grabbed my hand and led me down the stairs. "Come."

Making our way through the partygoers, Berri didn't let go until we reached a wet bar that had been set up on the lawn. Standing at the bar was a garrulous bear of a man in his sixties who was stirring a cocktail glass with his finger. He took a drink from the glass, then squirted it out through his front teeth into the bushes.

Lovely.

"Fucking vodka gimlet tastes like tap water," he scolded the bartender and handed the glass back to him. "Gimme a Scotch Rickey and this time try making it a long pour."

While he awaited his drink, he grabbed a handful of nuts from a bowl and shoved them in his mouth. Some made it, most didn't.

Berri came up and stood behind him, making it look like it would take two of her to equal one of him. Maybe more. She poked him in the back.

He turned around to look, giving Berri a big smile upon seeing her. All in, he must've weighed close to 250 pounds, his beady eyes sunk deep in a lantern-jawed face.

"Hey! What brings you here?" he said. He enveloped Berri in a huge hug, while I nervously listened close to see if I could hear bones breaking.

"To make sure you're on your best behavior," she said.

"Fat fucking chance there," he snickered.

I've always felt awkward around people I don't know, especially ones I don't want to know, but for some reason Berri wanted me to meet this guy. Standing off to the side, I uneasily shifted back and forth on my feet, something I did when I was uncomfortable. Some people said it gave them motion sickness.

"I have someone I want you to meet," Berri said as she reached back to bring me into the fold. "This is Emma Connolly, she's a rapturous new artist I just bought a painting from. Emma, this is Lenny Dusan. He owns the Czymanek Gallery in Old Town."

Lenny extended a giant paw of a hand, which I gingerly shook for fear of getting mine crushed.

"Hi, nice to meet you," I said in a voice that I was worried might've sounded more like a question.

The bartender handed Lenny his drink. "Here you go, sir."

Lenny took a huge swig and let out a satisfied gasp. "Now that's an old-school pour. Keep that shit flowing and you'll be my new best friend." He shoved $50 in the bartender's tip jar.

Well, at least his generosity matched his crassness. The only thing really missing from his repertoire at this point was either picking his teeth with a matchbook cover or floating an air biscuit.

He opted for the former, grabbing a toothpick and digging in, accompanied by random sucking sounds. When he finally finished his dental excavation, he turned his attention back to me.

"An artist, huh? Like we don't have enough of those already, right?" he laughed. "Just kidding."

"Her work is quite singular," Berri said.

"What kind of stuff do you do?" Lenny asked me.

"Acrylics," I answered.

"I was talking to Emma about having her own exhibition and I told her your gallery would be ideal," Berri added.

I'm sorry, but did I black out at some point and miss part of the festivities? What the fuck was she talking about?

Berri discreetly winked at me.

"Oh yeah? Do you paint nudes? Those always sell," Lenny said.

I couldn't tell if he was serious or just acting like a true man of culture. For whatever reason, he struck as a #MeToo case waiting to happen.

Berri rolled her eyes. "Someone's being boorish."

"Who, me?" Lenny said, although I was certain he didn't have a self-reflective bone in his entire Bigfoot-sized body.

Realizing this was an opening to unleash my devastating wit, I ventured forth. "Actually, I used to, but I kept getting busted on obscenity charges, so I switched."

That got a laugh from Lenny. Score one for homegirl.

Lenny stifled a small belch and touched his chest.

"Fucking arrhythmia is killing me," he griped.

"Well, before you die, how about you at least consider it?" Berri said, although I had no idea why she was pressing. I was barely fit for human consumption, let alone for a public showing. Oh, that and the fact that I basically had nothing to show.

Minor matters.

"Couldn't be worse than the last couple of bookings we've had. Total shit. Makes you want to close up and move to Antigua," Lenny said.

He took another large gulp of his drink, then looked at me and shrugged. "Yeah, what the hell. I trust Berri's taste. I'll take a look at what you have. Now, if you'll excuse me, I've gotta go drop a deuce."

An eloquent exit line, to be sure, as Lenny walked away to continue to spread his own unique brand of homespun charm.

I turned to Berri. "He owns an art gallery? Seems more like your average teamster."

"He's worth millions."

"Oh, well, that explains it then."

"Money doesn't buy class, but it does buy you exception."

I was hesitant to bring up the fact that my remaining artistic output was a little on the meager side, but then I thought if someone is going to vouch for me, I had to be like all upfront and shit.

"I have to be honest. I don't have anything near enough to warrant a showing."

Berri looked at me and smiled.

"I'm merely planting a seed, the rest is up to you, but let me give you one word, my dear. Immersion."

Finch and I stayed until the food ran out, always the last call for any party. We drove back to town and on the way, he told me that after talking to Bolan he'd come up with a great idea for his blog. He wanted to do an interview with him, keeping Bolan anonymous of course, about the vanishing breed of independent weed dealer and call it "Death of a Salesman." He seemed genuinely excited about it, and it sounded promising. His writing was great and I was sure he'd give it his own unique spin.

My mind, meanwhile, was occupied with the idea of ramping up my own output now. The groundwork had been laid for something I'd never even entertained as being possible, yet here it was. I realized I needed to do something I hadn't done in years.

Challenge myself.

Twelve

I've always had a long, tortured relationship with opportunity. I think it all started when I had the chance to skip second grade. I remember telling my parents in no uncertain terms that I did not want to leave my friends behind to go be plopped down with a random bunch of strangers. Not to mention the pure culture shock I was sure to endure by going from second to third grade.

At least it seemed that way in my preadolescent mind. After much debate, or at least as much as an eight-year-old could muster (I think it was more like morose pouting), I stayed put.

Somehow word had gotten out, though, that I'd been considered for being skipped, and even though I'd said no, a lot of my classmates turned on me. *Et tu*, Timmy? I guess they didn't like the fact that I was somehow above them, which I wasn't. It led to a lot of lunches by myself and when you're that age, something like that can really fuck up your already whisker-thin confidence.

Ever since then, I've always been somewhat wary of opportunities. As a result, a lot of my silver linings always came with rain.

So here was another chance presenting itself yet again, although the prospect of showing what I could do artistically now as an adult seemed so unlikely, I barely allowed it to register.

The best way to describe how I felt after the party was if you've ever been to a really great concert, you feel totally adrenalized after it's over, convinced you can now go kick the world squarely in the balls. By the time you got home, however, and PCD (post-concert depression) had settled in, you'd reverted to the funk of your own life.

That was me, so naturally, I embraced this new opportunity the best way I knew how. I backslid.

For the next three weeks, my life consisted of work, gaming, and seeing Finch on a regular basis.

And no painting.

It was almost as if that big bash hadn't happened. When Mr. Spangler was here, I had a definitive goal, but now left to my own defective devices, there was no pressure being applied. I pretty much felt like a sloth on vacation.

I also got fed up with looking at the mess in my living room, as it was still set up as some quasi-studio, so a cleanup on Aisle 5 seemed the right call. I spent three hours breaking everything down and packing it up. Once that was done, the only thing left was to put my paintings somewhere.

I briefly gave thought to hanging them on the wall, but that seemed just so incredibly narcissistic. If someone came over and commented on them, what was I supposed to do, casually mention, "Oh yes, I did those. Fancy a spot of tea? I'll ring the servants."

I decided the living room closet made the most sense. I carried the paintings over, set them down outside the door, and just stood there. Call it paranoia, but I had the strangest feeling Mr. Spangler was going to be waiting inside, furious at me for not keeping my word, and we'd start all over again.

I tried to force myself to open the door.

Could. Not. Do. It.

I had become totally paralyzed by irrational thinking. Not an uncommon occurrence for me, but this one truly stood out. Besides, it was really crowded in there to begin with. I'd be better off taking them down to storage with the other stuff. Yeah, that sounded good.

God, what a fucking world-class talent I had for taking away my own will.

I rented the same U-Haul van that I had used when I bought the supplies, but now I was headed down to stow them away at the most terrifying place on Earth.

Public storage.

North Korea, Libya, Iraq, they're all holiday destinations compared to the horrors that await you at one of these facilities with their long, eerie hallways, strange noises, and hostile employees. Behind every locked door I assumed there was either a meth lab or a dead body, which is why I always went right when the facility opened. That way, I figured most of the freakazoid renters were still in lock-up.

I signed in and gave them my driver's license in exchange for a rickety cart with a busted wheel, which I never thought was a fair swap. Here you were giving them personal information for some beaten-up, POS equipment. Who knew what they were going to do with your info while you were off negotiating those dimly lit corridors? True, they had all your vitals the moment you first signed up, but why remind them? Okay, forget it. I just talked myself out of my own argument.

I stacked everything on the cart and hauled it down to my already overstuffed unit. I'd had the place for a couple of years, and it'd become the great dumping ground for things I knew I was going to eventually throw away, but just hadn't developed the full emotional disconnect for yet. Miraculously, it all fit with a minimum of reconfiguration.

I started to close the door and got a last glimpse of the paintings.

They were really pretty fucking good. And I decided to leave it at that. Why?

Fill in the blank. Fear of failure, fear of success, procrastination, or its ugly stepchild, laziness. They all work.

Jesus, I felt like such an asshole now for criticizing that girl Sheridan at the party for her laundry list of excuses, and here I was doing the same thing. I wasn't a big, fat hypocrite, I was a morbidly obese one.

As I locked up, I noticed a woman in her late forties down the hall from me had dragged the contents of her storage locker, mostly clothing, out into the hallway. She was tall and lithe and reminded me of a ballet teacher I once had when I was in grade school, minus the stick and fascist attitude. As she went through the pile, she paused to either touch or smell each item as if to evoke some type of sense memory.

She looked up and saw me waiting with my cart.

"Oh, I'm sorry. Let me get this out of the way for you."

"Thanks."

She tried to clear a path, jamming her belongings back into the small locker, although a lot kept falling back out, frustrating her to no end. She finally looked at me almost beggingly. "You want any of this stuff, you can have it."

"No thanks. Got way too much of my own to go through."

"It's just going to get tossed."

I noticed that a lot of her clothes weren't the average stuff you'd stash in storage just because you'd gotten bored with it. She held up a gorgeous leopard print raglan sweater.

"Never worn," she teased.

"Is that Juicy?" I asked.

"No, but thanks. I designed it myself."

"Really? It's beautiful."

"Wish everyone thought the way you do," she sighed.

I walked over to her and bent down to look at the clothes scattered on the floor.

"All of this is really nice. Why would you want to throw it away?"

"Ghosts," she replied.

I snapped straight up. Okay, this was getting bizarre. Other people had the same problems too? Christ, was there a paranormal pandemic going around?

"I tried to start my own clothing line a few years ago and it failed. Miserably. I lost a small fortune. Worst decision I've ever made. I've been trying to sell off pieces, pennies on the dollar, but even that seems to have finally dried up, so I'm left with a lot of this stuff that just haunts me."

"How about selling it online?"

"Tried that. Dribs and drabs. Nothing."

"What about donating it?"

"I suppose," she said. "Tell you the truth, I'd rather just be done with it."

There was something about the way she carried herself, her voice and whole demeanor, that I found sad. Defeated.

"I don't know. Maybe you're right," she reconsidered. "Might as well give someone good use of it."

"Absolutely," I chirped.

"You sure you don't want anything?"

Bottom feeder that I was, I couldn't resist. I picked up the sweater. "May I?"

"Be my guest," she said.

"Thanks. Listen, I know there's a Brown Elephant just about five blocks away."

"I'll make it my next stop," she smiled.

"Good luck," I said, although in retrospect that was probably a stupid thing to say to someone who'd already failed.

Convinced I'd done my good deed for the day, I took my cart back to the main office and signed out. As I got in the van, Finch called and we spent the next fifteen minutes deciding where to go that night. We finally settled on doing the two-hour Segway tour of the city, even though neither of us had ever been on one before. The first one to do a face plant had to buy dinner.

While I sat in the parking lot talking to him, I noticed that the woman I'd met inside had come out with a cart piled high with her clothes. She proceeded to wheel over to a nearby dumpster and started chucking everything in the bin.

What the fuck? I was pissed. She had totally rejected my suggestion of donating them, even after she said she would. When she'd finally thrown the last batch in, she stared into the bin for a few moments, then pushed her cart back into the building.

I hung up with Finch and sat there in the van, debating whether to go dumpster-diving because this was just insane. I got out and walked over to the bin and looked inside. Any thoughts of saving the discarded threads were immediately ended when I saw most were sitting on top of some black tarry shit. A few items seemed salvageable, but they were way in the back and would've required me hopping in and rooting around like a fucking raccoon scrounging for food.

As I walked back to the van, I got angrier and angrier at the total waste. It flashed through my mind to go back in and call her out for what she did.

Instead, I got back in the van and just sat there.

Thinking.

I finally came to the ugly conclusion that in an odd way, how different was I than her? Yes, I had kept the fruits of my labor, but I guess I was dwelling on the idea of just abandoning something you created. Jesus, was this going to be me in a couple of years? Would I wind up tossing everything too? What if I dropped dead or got hit by the L and someone had to clean out my unit? What would they think, besides that I kept the most meaningless junk. And what would they say when they found my paintings?

In high school, I studied poetry and how Emily Dickinson had virtually all her work discovered after she died. Talk about being born at the wrong time. With all the creative platforms there are today, she'd have blown up big time. She would've started her own webpage and gotten millions of hits, developed a cult following, eventually landed a lucrative book deal, been picked for *Time*'s 100 Most Influential List, followed by the inevitable social media backlash, gotten slapped with charges of plagiarism, and eventually gone through a bitter divorce and custody battle. Fuck it, she's better off dead.

The more I thought about it, I realized it would suck to be defined by regret, and that idea just kept gnawing at me, saying that was what I was setting myself up for. To the best of my limited knowledge, they didn't give out awards for failure or else a lot of people's trophy case shelves would be buckling with achievements.

So rather than kneel to that, I decided to do something unique to me.

I reversed course.

I went back inside the storage building, got the cart again, and returned to my unit. I dragged out all the stuff I had just put in, stacked it on the cart, and wheeled it back out to load up in the van.

I was giving myself a mulligan for bailing on things.

Why?

Because for once, I knew it was the right choice to make.

When I returned the cart, I ran into the woman with the clothes at the front desk, where she was finalizing her move out of the building. I didn't mention anything though, because really, what was I going to say? Confronting her for what she did would've just seemed like piling on at that point. As she gathered up her paperwork and left the office, she saw me and smiled. I smiled back. Nothing was said, and as I watched her walk away, I flashed on the tired cliché that as one door closes, another one opens.

Hang on, does that still apply when it's between two people? Shit, now I'm going to overanalyze it. Well, either way, somehow her resignation had led to my re-inspiration and this time I was determined not to fuck it up.

I got the apartment back in fighting shape, like my creative hiccup never happened.

The big question was how many more pieces would I need to come up with for a showing. I devoured any information I could find on the internet, made calls, and then finally went down and looked at the size of the gallery that I hopefully was going to be dealing with.

I decided not to go in, because to me out of sight was out of mind. If I reintroduced myself, it might give the enchanting Lenny an extra chance to change his mind even before seeing my work. I was more about the surprise attack, saying, "Remember me, motherfucker? BAM, here I am."

The gallery was a medium-sized space, so I figured I'd need at least another good ten to twelve paintings to make the best use of it. I initially thought, well, there goes my summer, but shockingly I was able to finish what I wanted in about six weeks for one simple reason.

I had decided to give myself a complete life hack.

For a month and a half, I did nothing but work and paint. That was it. No gaming and no weed to distract me. At first, I thought I'd have to go through some twelve-step for pot-smoking gamers, but I was amazed at how easy it was for me to convert inertia into obsessional focus. I tried to employ a semi-healthy diet too, which I'm sure drove the employees at my nearby Shake Shack into bereavement.

Finch and I hung out on some weekends, although not at my place. I was too embarrassed by what a complete mess it'd become as a result of my reignited compulsion. Worse than ever before. He seemed fine with my schedule and, more importantly, totally supportive of how much I wanted to flip the script.

It was a brutally hot June night when my convulsive air conditioner finally decided to fuck off and die, leaving me sitting on a stool, dripping sweat. I was putting the finishing touches on a painting of a group of bulls with neon-colored horns floating through space that I was going to call "*Glo-bull.*" When I was satisfied it was what I wanted, I put the brush down and stepped back to look. I never used the word "done," paintings were never done, there were only degrees of contentment. I moved to different angles, because to me art had to capture your attention not just from standing directly in front of it. Pleased with the work, I heaved out a deep sigh.

I had reached my goal. A dozen paintings of various shapes and sizes sat spread out in a semi-circle around me, and as I looked at them, all I could do was grab my head in disbelief.

I fucking did it.

It represented the single biggest accomplishment I had ever achieved in my time taking up space on the planet. Strangely enough, I kept thinking about how Mr. Spangler never got a chance to see these. After all, he was the one who gave me the initial kick in the ass.

I think he would've been proud.

Needing to decompress, I invited Finch over for the weekend. I was anxious to know what he thought, even though I was sure he wouldn't be objective, which was okay. I could use a little positivity before my paintings were possibly thrown to the wolves. My apartment had now returned to normal, like the final segment of *Hoarders,* minus the come-to-Jesus moment.

I answered the door and Finch stood in the hallway with a bouquet of purple hyacinths (my all-time fave), wine, and a wicker basket of fruit and cheese. He stuck his arm out holding the flowers.

"Here, hurry, take 'em. I'm about to bust out in hives."

I grabbed the flowers and pulled Finch in. I closed the door and was promptly all over him like a feral cat in heat. I hadn't seen him for a couple of weeks, and there was only so much sexting and phonebone one could do.

"Miss me?" he said between gulps of air.

"To be determined," I breathed in his ear.

We staggered over to the kitchen counter, still locked up, yet somehow managed to land everything on the countertop. We then lurched out to the living room couch, where I fell on top of him and we tore at each other's clothes until Finch suddenly let out a piercing howl.

"What?" I panicked.

He sat up and looked behind him, pulling out a palette knife that somehow had gotten stuck between the cushions.

Blood was soon to follow.

I spent the next fifteen minutes playing nurse, tending to the cut that the knife had made in Finch's back. I felt terrible and kept apologizing over and over. He wanted to see what he thought for sure was a gaping wound, but I kept reassuring him it was nothing.

"C'mon, how bad is it?" he asked.

It was time to fess up. "You're lucky. It just missed puncturing a lung."

"What??"

He turned and looked at me, a smile on my face.

"It's fine," I said. I finished doctoring him and kissed his newly bandaged back. "You're good to go."

He sat up and pulled his shirt back on, then looked around the apartment.

"Where are all your paintings?" he asked.

I hopped off the couch and seductively motioned him with my finger. He stood up and followed me down the hall.

"Ooh, I'm liking this," he said.

When we walked into the bedroom, he had his answer. Laid out against the walls were all my paintings. Finch looked a little confused.

"Why are they in here?"

"Because I want this to be the last thing I see when I go to sleep, and the first thing I see when I wake up. I need to remind myself of where I want to be."

"This is nuts. How many do you have total?"

"Sixteen," I answered. There I was with that whole infinity thing again, this time eight doubled. I had read one lousy book on numerology five years ago, and now it had fucked me up for life. Something tells me I'd probably be choice cult recruitment material.

Finch was duly impressed by the paintings, but like I said, I think he viewed them with a bias. He seemed to genuinely dig the whole surrealistic motif and was convinced they'd go over big. Truth? I wish he'd been a little more reserved in his praise, not because I didn't know how to handle a compliment, but because I *really* didn't know how to handle a compliment.

We spent the whole weekend in bed, only taking turns to answer the door when food delivery showed up. I don't think I'd ever felt closer to Finch than I did those two days, but thankfully neither one of us felt compelled to start dropping L-bombs to fuck things up.

As they always do.

On Sunday morning I was curled up next to him, trying to braid his chest hair, and flattered he was being so inquisitive about where my ideas came from, how long each one took, etc. One of the things I adored about Finch was his curiosity. Not just about me, but about the world at large. Nothing crashed a relationship faster than being with someone whose most incisive question was whether I put the toilet paper over or under.

I was trying to explain my process but doing a miserable job of it.

"I don't know. I just couldn't believe how fast I was creating. I've never felt that alive in my life. I just had this incredible energy flowing through me," I effused. "I'm still kinda feeling that way."

"I believe it. I think I was just the recipient of a little of the runoff."

I reached down and gave Finch an unscheduled testicular exam.

"Ouch, party foul," he barked.

"No, I'm serious. I was on fire. The whole world melted away and I was going on pure instinct. It reminded me of when I was younger. I used to say painting was like fishing with dynamite because it was so effortless for me."

Finch softly kissed me on the forehead. "Ya done good."

"Thanks."

I reached over to fire up a fatty. It would be the first one I'd had in seemingly forever, and a perfect way to start the day.

"Hey, that reminds me, I finished the article I wrote about Bolan. Wanna read it?"

I sat up, excited. "Of course I want to read it! How was he to interview?"

"He was interesting. Told me many, many lurid stories about you."

I laughed as I took a hit. "Yeah, they never happened."

"I think he's the type of guy who could do anything he wanted, if he set his mind to it."

"Absolutely. Just needs motivation like the rest of us," I said.

I read Finch's blog over lunch and there was a ton of shit in there about Bolan I never knew, like he was engaged once, and even robbed at gunpoint. Maybe it was the kind of thing where guys opened up more to other guys, but you'd still think I would've heard. The article was fascinating, and I could tell that Bolan was definitely phasing out of the business. He did come across as somewhat adrift, but it ended on an optimistic note that he was looking forward to the next chapter in his life.

It was easily the best thing I'd read by Finch, and I told him so. I know it might've sounded like we had a mutual strokefest going on, but our admiration was genuine. That's how you know when things are working. Unwavering support and great sex are always the cornerstones of any solid relationship.

Maybe not in that order.

I spent most of the next week photographing the paintings for a portfolio that I needed to put together. Dumbass me thought you just dragged all your stuff down in person and got a thumbs up or thumbs down, but portfolios were de rigueur now for galleries. I had scheduled to meet Lenny on Tuesday after work, and I insisted Finch come along for moral support. Well, that and the fact I wanted someone to get drunk with to either celebrate or commiserate the verdict.

I got down to the gallery about thirty minutes before closing. I sat nervously holding my portfolio outside Lenny's office while he was on the phone. His assistant, Rosario, couldn't have been sweeter. She offered me words of encouragement and basically every beverage ever made, including Green River, the only soda that matters.

Finally, after about twenty minutes of waiting (grrr!) Lenny came out to greet me.

"Sorry about that, I couldn't get off the call," he said.

"No problem." Yes, there fucking was, but I buried my irritation.

Rosario came over and handed him a stack of messages. "Kurt from the auction house just called. Says he absolutely must speak to you today."

"Tell that prick he can wait."

"Of course, but in a more diplomatic way," Rosario said.

"Why?" Lenny said to her. He motioned me to follow him over to a large work table.

"Remind me where we met again," he said.

"The party in Lake Forest. Berri introduced us."

"Oh right, right. You're Berri's friend. God, I love her. A real original. She's like the sister I never wanted."

He stopped at the table and put out his balloon-sized hand. "Let's see what we're working with here."

I gave him my portfolio, which he unzipped and spread open on the table. My stomach was doing cartwheels as he flipped through the photos with little to no reaction. Not exactly what you'd call promising. He did cock his head to look at one of them, but that was hardly a tell.

"Who else have you shown these to?" he asked.

"No one."

"Are you selling on the internet?"

"No."

"Okay," he said as he finished looking through the portfolio and closed it up. "So, what do you want from me?"

Uh, end hunger and world peace?

"I was hoping to get an exhibition for my work."

"I'm not interested in people who hope. People who play the lottery 'hope' they win. Is that you? You 'want' to get an exhibition. Big difference. Are you locally based?"

"Born and bred."

"Here's what we do here. Exhibitions are usually booked for two to four weeks, we take care of framing and PR, but if you want to put it on blast on your own social media, that's great. Anything to drive traffic in here. I decide which pieces get shown, and the gallery takes 40 percent of all sales. After it's over, you come get your stuff. We're not a damn storage facility. Always have to tell artists that. If I like you, I might ask you back. Do consider yourself lucky because I'm talking to you, as we don't take open submissions. There's a bunch of other stuff, but if I decide to go with you, I'll have Rosario fill you in."

"Got it."

"Your stuff is interesting, I'll give you that."

"Thanks."

"Which counts for about 60 percent with me."

"What's the other 40 percent?"

"You. I don't have a curator. I choose everything that goes on these walls. And I choose that based in part on what I think of the artist. Look, I'm an asshole, and you know why?"

I did everything in my power to keep from blurting out, "Second nature?"

"Because it keeps the weak away. I don't hand hold or babysit, I don't have time for it. But I do invest in people. Sometimes I'm right, sometimes I'm wrong. I'd say I'm about 70 percent on target. Go on the internet, a lot of artists hate me. 'Abrasive, crass, insensitive,' you'll find it all, but keep scrolling until you start finding different opinions. Find the ex-gangbanger whose urban art exhibit here jump-started a career, or the recovering mixed-media artist who changed her life after a two-week showing, or the vet coming off three tours of duty who sold $5K worth of photos in a month here. They all love my rude ass. You still interested?"

"Yes."

"Then that was just the appetizer. You're the meal. Follow me."

I trailed him into a smaller wing of the gallery, as he pointed at a watercolor exhibition that lined the walls. "You think your work is better than this?" he said.

I tried to be diplomatic. "I'm probably the wrong person to ask. I'm not a big watercolor fan."

"Neither am I. But do you know what this is?"

Jesus, I felt like I was a grunt in basic training. I knew I had to hang tough, though. He hadn't said no yet.

"No idea."

"This is a month-long favor and I'm dying with it. Now Berri wants a favor. What am I supposed to do?"

I looked at the paintings again. "Don't book any more watercolor exhibitions?"

Lenny chuckled and nodded. "Forever."

"And yes, I think what I have is better," I said.

"So sell me. Why should it be you up here?" he said, gesturing at the walls.

"I let the paintings sell me. I'm just the name on them."

"That's a nice canned answer, but what's your story?"

Say what you like about Lenny, and obviously many people already had, but he was direct and in your face. No matter how churlish he seemed, there was no bullshit about him. The more I talked to him, the more I liked that. Maybe he was the type who made a better first impression the second time you met them.

I paused for a moment, weighing what to say. Something told me he wasn't going to care anyway, so I might as well vent. It'd make me feel better.

"My story? Which part?" I said.

"The part that makes me say yes."

"Well, do you want the first twenty years where everything was about creating art and filling my head with dreams? Or do you want the last seven, where I've been chasing myself down a rabbit hole?"

"And what about now?"

"Honestly? I have no idea about now, except everything you saw in that portfolio represents a total recommitment. A complete 180 from where I was. And why should it be me? Because I think my work deserves to be seen, but if it isn't me, I'll be cool with that because it's not going to stop me. I'm going to get it all back. Every fucking thing I left behind."

Lenny stared at me, sizing me up. He did not look impressed. At all.

I came out of the gallery in a daze, not quite sure what had just happened. I looked around for Finch and found him doing donuts in the parking lot with those horrible electric scooters the city had plagued us with. He saw me and docked the scooter, then came over with an excited look on his face.

"Well??" he asked.

I was still trying to process as I blindly handed him my portfolio, then crouched down and let out a massive scream. I mean a real Chester Bennington shriek.

People walking nearby looked over to see if I was okay. Finch waved at them.

"She's fine. She just got a parking ticket. They're so unfair."

I looked up at Finch, trying to catch my breath.

"I got in," I panted, with no air left in my lungs.

We went to a nearby wine bar where we overdosed on Manzanilla and tapas. I was still trying to wrap my mind around the meeting.

"Fuck me running, how does this even happen?"

"Why? What did he say?" said Finch.

"I thought I was dead meat. It was just this feeling I got. Complete disinterest on his part. Then I started talking about myself, and out of nowhere he says he can offer me a two-week slot at the end of August. He said he likes to be proven correct. No pressure, right?"

I chugged the sediments out of the bottom and was ready to start chewing on the glass.

"I'm sure the paintings had a lot to do with his decision," Finch declared.

"He said they were different and that they hadn't had much in the way of surrealism for a while. I guess that helped."

"C'mon, Em, you don't get offered a showing because of your personality, as sweetly acidic as it may be. I told you that your stuff was great," said Finch.

I looked at him with a glazed-over stare. "Yeah, but Finch...now what?"

Thirteen

The answer to that question came in a laundry list of things I had to plan for the opening night of the exhibition. First up was to put together an invite list, which I initially assumed would be huge, but as I started to organize it, I was shocked at how anemic it really was. It included all the obvious choices: my parents, Finch, some people I knew from work, Bolan, Berri, and that writer I had met at the party. I even reached out to Natalie, even though she was 1300 miles away. Was my world really that minuscule? Death row inmates had bigger pen pal lists than I had contacts. And if that wasn't sobering enough, the response was even more deflating.

Mom said she was going to be recovering from vaginal rejuvenation surgery the week of the opening and didn't want to travel. She swore she'd send flowers, said she was so proud of me, always believed in my talent (cough...cough...bullshit), while the rest of our conversation dissolved into white noise.

Dad said he would try and make it, but I wasn't going to hold out much hope. I'm guessing a major MMA or Brazilian Jiu-Jitsu tournament he was in would eventually keep him away.

Here's where the correction and retraction portion comes in handy.

I originally said I wasn't bothered by the fact that our little nuclear family of three weren't all that close-knit when I was growing up. It did bother me, but I didn't let it, if that makes any sense. I suppose I had so steeled myself from disappointment over the years with my parents, that I had gotten to the point where I looked at our dysfunction as just being normal.

I gave Natalie more of a pass because of the distance, and the fact she had a trade show in Miami the week of my opening.

It was looking like it'd just be me and Finch and whatever drunks we could bribe to stagger in from the bar next door.

Next, I had to write my artist's statement. This was going to be printed in the program that would be handed out at the gallery, and was supposed to represent who I was, why I chose to make my art the way I did, and what I was trying to accomplish.

After much soul-searching, this is what I came up with.

"My name is Emma Connolly and thank you for attending the first exhibition of my work. Never in a million years would I have envisioned being in such a position, especially when you consider what a fuck up I've been for so long. Try being on the bong and a video game addict for over half a decade and let me know what you achieve. Until recently, I've also made horrible choices in men, which I'm sure didn't help my self-esteem. I've also been told I can be prickly and judgmental, yet I look at those as positives.

The work you see before you represents the totally deranged way I see much of the world. Full of absurdity and incongruities. Yes, it's been that way since childhood for me. I suppose it's my way of coping with things I have no control over. I'm not trying for any grandiose message with my work, so if you see some great meaning in something I've painted, you're probably full of shit and are very annoying. Go away.

Finally, my main goal with my work is to entertain and provoke thought. If you don't feel that way, I'll probably sink into a deep depression, so feel free to lie. Thank you for coming and please buy a lot. I could really use the money."

Says it all, right? Of course, my real artist's statement wound up being some generic treatise that read like a stockholder's report, but hey, kids, isn't it fun to pretend?!

While the gallery was going to provide a bar, it was my responsibility to come up with the nosh. Naturally that meant I'd be spending long, painstaking hours right up until the last minute making just-perfect finger foods.

In an alternate universe.

I called a local caterer and got a quote of $500 for a spread, which I thought was a bit pricey, but I'd heard you had a better chance at sales if your attendees were stuffed and drunk.

God bless impaired decision-making.

I finally came out of my bunker regarding social media, albeit kicking and screaming. Finch and his roommate, Craig, helped me set up my own personal webpage that linked to the gallery. Jesus, now I was like every other self-aggrandizing hustler out there and I hated it, but such were the necessary evils if you wanted to be considered professional. After about two weeks of the site being up and running, I finally stopped going to it. I became obsessed with always checking the hit counter and responding to idiotic comments people were leaving asking how long I was going to be visiting Earth, what was my weed strain of choice, and whether or not I liked anal.

The last and potentially most difficult thing I needed to do was find the right clothes to wear for opening night. When I first started looking up advice, I became very excited. I repeatedly read things like, "Wear clothes that let people know who you are and reflect your own personal style." This is great, I thought, I could show up in sweatpants and my grungy *Life Is Strange* T-shirt. Shit, I'd even wash it! Sadly, though, I realized the gamer uni would be a no-go as I needed to show a modicum of maturity.

This meant I had to go shopping because I could find nothing in my wardrobe that screamed "*Artiste!*" I haunted the boutiques in Bucktown until, three hours later, I came away with a black lace-embellished jumpsuit. The reason it took so long was that I thought everything I looked at would work, but after about five minutes I realized I hated whatever clothes I had with me, put them back, and started again. The jumpsuit won by attrition, but I was genuinely happy with it. I think.

Someday, when I become age-appropriate, I want to have children. I know I'd be a good mom, although I probably wouldn't handle the whole kid-leaving-home scenario so well. Pouring eighteen years of your heart and soul into someone only to have them bail on you seems like a fucked up rate of return. I mention this because in a funny way, I got a preview of that when the gallery called for my paintings.

As I boxed them up, I realized that if everything broke right I'd never be seeing some of them again. I had grown umbilically connected to my work, which I know wasn't a healthy thing to do if you were creating for public consumption.

After leaving the paintings off, I thought this is what that first day of college must be like for parents. As you wave goodbye, you hope things go great for your kid and four years later they come out whip-smart and ready to make a dent in the world. Or else they wind up like me.

I was now locked and loaded with my fate placed at the mercy of strangers, all of whom hopefully had exceptional taste.

The remaining weeks leading up to the opening seemed to drag on forever, the way school does when you're a kid. This left me plenty of time to second-guess what I had created. Was it good enough? Was it too obtuse? Did I spell my name right? I obsessed over the most inane details.

Finally, the big night had arrived. I got there way early just to make sure everything was perfect, but unfortunately, I soon found out my worst fears had been realized. Out of all the people I had invited, only Finch was going to make it. Color me so not fucking surprised.

The writer from the *Sentinel* had left me an email profusely apologizing for his being unable to attend, but swore he'd check out the website. Blah, blah, blah. Lenny told me Berri was also going to be a no-show, which really hurt considering she was a large part of why I was here in the first place. Bolan said he'd stop by, but I wasn't going to hold my breath, and earlier in the day, I had gotten a call from my dad. He'd broken his leg in a lacrosse tournament, and he didn't think he'd be good company wobbling around in a cast and crutches. To be expected. I had basically succeeded in repelling one and all.

I took it all in stride, determined not to let anything ruin the night for me. Fuck everyone who blew me off, I thought. I was determined to shine, no matter what. The turnout was shockingly decent, as the gallery had done a good job of promoting the opening. As Finch and I watched people arrive, I noticed it was a nice mix of hipsters and what seemed like seasoned gallery denizens. We wandered among the crowd, trying to overhear what people were saying. I couldn't get a read on things yet, but the picture suddenly began to darken as I heard the loud thud of skin against skin. A woman screamed, and I looked over at two men who were beating the living shit out of each other.

It was hardly proper gallery etiquette.

The smaller of the two hollered, "You don't know what the hell you're talking about!" The pair wrestled each other to the floor and continued to rabbit-punch each other. People quickly stepped in to try and pull them apart.

As if that wasn't bad enough, out of the far corner of the gallery wing, a man started yelling. Not at another person, but at one of the paintings. The guy looked like he'd lost his mind, as he was doing full primal scream therapy at a canvas of acrylics.

Uh, security, anyone?

The whole atmosphere of the room had quickly changed as voices began to rise in loud discussions. I was glad the work was stimulating conversation, but this wasn't the floor of the Chicago Mercantile Exchange, for fuck's sake.

A woman stormed over and shoved the program at me. "You, you're the artist, right?"

"Yes, I am," I replied.

"What the hell does this mean?" she said. She jabbed her corpulent finger toward a painting of a group of small beds hanging upside down from a ceiling, while a group of infants slept on the floor below. I had called the piece "*Cot Up*," but for whatever reason, she was not digging it.

"It's a play on words," I explained.

"That's not how you spell caught, and do you think this is any way to treat children?" she fumed.

I was having a major WTF moment with this Karen.

"Yeah, this shit is disgusting," piped in another man as he walked over to join our little impromptu focus group.

"It's garbage!" screamed a voice from somewhere in the gallery.

"Get her!" bellowed another less-than-pleased attendee.

Immediately, a crowd of people had surrounded me, pulling on my arms, my hair, and any other appendage readily available.

Finch tried to yank me free but got knocked back. One of his piercings came loose in the fracas, and he dove on the floor trying to find it.

"I think I saw it roll under the bench over there," I yelled to him.

"Thanks!" he said and began immediate pursuit.

Meanwhile, the crowd dragged me outside to the alley, where there was a makeshift bonfire ready to go. They hauled me to the top of the heap and lit that sucker up. As the flames crackled and the bloodthirsty crowd raucously cheered, all I could flash on was what a bitch it was gonna be getting the smoke out of my jumpsuit.

I awakened just before I turned into a complete crispy critter and sat up in bed thinking one thing and one thing only.

I am never fucking smoking Tahoe Alien before going to bed again.

I got a call from Lenny a few days before the opening (the *real* opening), telling me that everything was framed and to come look at the layout. When I got there, my first disappointment was that I was getting the smaller wing of the gallery, not the main area, but I understood why. Basically, first-timers had to take what they were given and STFU. I stood there staring at my paintings, which had been beautifully framed, and I almost felt like crying.

This was actually happening. To me.

That emotional rush was short-lived, however, as the second disappointment arrived with the news that only twelve of my paintings were going to be on display. Lenny said this was done primarily because of space, and that he felt it was just the right amount to generate interest, citing how you never want to bludgeon people with overkill. That left four orphans, although they would be available on the website and in the program. I deferred to his expertise, although I think he could tell I was a little miffed at the decision.

Surprisingly, we had no problem agreeing on the pricing, as I let sugar plum dollar signs dance in my head. The reality, of course, was I just hoped I'd be able to pay all my bills on time after the whole thing was over. I thanked Lenny for everything he'd done so far, he wished me good luck, and I came out of there on a natural high that carried me through the rest of the week.

Common sense dictated that I needed a full eight hours of sleep the night before the opening so I'd be sharp and personable, a suggestion that my brain promptly told to get fucked.

I got four hours tops. I simply could not shut off.

How could you sleep on the eve of the biggest day of your life?

I mostly sat up in bed staring at nothing, while thinking about everything. I was about to call Finch to have him talk me down from the ledge of insomnia, but then thought better of it. I began to fade for good around 3 a.m., and when I finally woke up, the groggy aftermath had already taken root.

I knew it was going to be a long-ass day.

I dragged through work, but Hendu called me in the field and said I could knock off early because of the event. This was a blessing in disguise because it would allow me time to grab a quick mani-pedi, but instead I opted for a much-needed power nap.

In my car.

What the hell was it with me falling asleep in my Mini? It was like I had fucking carcolepsy or something.

On the way home I got a call from my dad. I could immediately tell from his voice that he wasn't coming, although the reason why was straight out of the strange-but-probably-true department. He had popped his ACL rock climbing at the gym the day before and spent today getting X-rays and adjusting to life with a knee brace. I felt totally guilty over this, knowing full well I'd cursed him with my dream.

I got back to my place with two hours to get ready. You may think that's a lot of time, and if you do, you're a guy. Sorry, it's not a shower, a shit, and a shave. It's a ritual. Luckily, my outfit was already chosen, so that left plenty of time for hair, makeup, and, most importantly, accessorizing. I pawed through my options, my bed looking like someone had dumped the entire contents of a steamer trunk filled with jewelry on it. I finally went with my old standby, a gorgeous Mae Statement necklace that I'd had since high school, a chunky gold belt, and a slap bracelet.

There I was. Ready to meet the world. Well, wait a minute now, that stretch cuff bracelet was gleaming at me. Maybe I should go with that.

A phone call from Finch broke up the possible stalemate.

"Hiya," I said.

"Hi, listen, I want to pick you up."

"Okay, why?"

"C'mon, it's your night. You're to do nothing but be smart, charming, and semi-alluring. And don't worry, I'm not driving the Deathmobile."

"Finch, I can't be late. Swear you'll be on time."

"I'll be there in twenty minutes. OnStar promised."

I felt a little uneasy about relying on Finch, not that he was habitually late, but I just felt better having my fate in my own hands.

"Let me know when you're here," I reluctantly agreed.

"Do you look smokin' hot?" he said in his best bedroom voice.

"Bye."

As I sat in the living room awaiting Finch's arrival, my mind began to wander. I was still staggered by how far my life had evolved over the past few months.

Wait, the word 'evolved' could finally be applied to me in a positive way. Happy dance!

Of course, none of this would've happened without the impetus of the man not in the room. I thought about that a lot as I waited, so much so that I finally felt compelled to call out loud, "Are you here?"

Silence.

Whatever. I figured it was worth a shot. I got a text from Finch telling me to meet him out front, so I grabbed my clutch, got up, and walked to the front door. I stopped and decided to try one last time, turning back to look at the empty living room.

"I'm leaving now."

Crickets.

"Well, this is all your fault," I said. "I hope you're happy."

And as I left, somehow I hoped he was.

When I came out in front of the apartment building, Finch was nowhere to be found. I was irked because I knew traffic would be a nightmare at this time on a Friday. I called him to voice my slight displeasure.

"Finch, where the fuck are you?"

"I'm almost there. I've hit every red light in the city."

"Look, I'll just drive myself."

"Wait, no!"

I heard a loud squeal of tires as a black sedan suddenly tore around the corner. The car screeched to a stop in front of me, Finch at the wheel. He nonchalantly got out and sauntered over, looking *très suave* in a gray sharkskin suit.

"See! I'm here," he said with a grin. "Wow, you look yummy. Can we have sex later?"

I pointed at the car. "What is this?"

"This is your transpo tonight."

"No, I mean where did you get it?"

"Ah, yes. All will be explained once you get inside."

"Fine. Let's go," I said and walked to the car.

Finch ducked around to open the door for me. It was locked. He yanked on the handle a couple of times, then took out the remote key. He tried to unlock it using that and succeeded in doing nothing but setting off the alarm.

I grabbed the key out of his hand, turned off the alarm, and unlocked the car. He graciously opened the door and motioned me inside with a sweeping gesture. At times, his charm was so endearingly cornball somebody could've bottled it and sold the shit.

I got inside and was immediately impressed by the pristine interior, great new car smell, and tons of legroom. This was one sweet-ass ride. Before this, I think the nicest car I'd ever ridden in was my old roomie's Passat, until it got stolen and stripped. That's right, only the best whips for me.

Finch climbed in and turned to me.

"So, what do you think of the car?"

"Definitely an upgrade. Where did you get it?"

"Well, first, the why. Shocking as it may seem, on some occasions I have been known to show class, tonight being one of them, so I rented this just for you."

"Thanks," I said, touched by his gentlemanly behavior.

"But here's the best part. I got the full rental insurance coverage on this so we can trash it later if we want. And speaking of surprises, I have something else for you. Close your eyes and put out your hands."

I shut my eyes and held out my hands. Knowing Finch, I half expected a live animal to be dropped in my palms.

"Ready?"

"Yes," I said.

"No peeking."

"I won't"

"Promise?"

I opened my eyes and gave Finch one of my trademarked "Stop with the bullshit" looks.

"Okay, okay," said Finch.

I closed my eyes again and felt something placed in my hands.

"You can look."

I opened my eyes and there was a small velvet bag. "What is it?" I asked.

"That's why it's called a surprise."

Here's a tip. Don't surprise me. Ever. I always want to know ahead of time. It helps me function. And yes, I always read the endings of books first.

I opened the bag and peeled through multiple layers of tissue paper until I finally uncovered a diamond nose stud. I looked at it closely.

"Is this for reals?"

Finch nodded. "Absolutely. I thought you might like an upgrade."

My jaw dropped. I couldn't believe it. "Oh my God, Finch. This is gorgeous. Thank you."

Let's recap. Up until this point, I think the best gift I'd ever gotten was a Nickelodeon cartoon watch on my eighth birthday. My first one ever. It might not have seemed like much, but that watch said to me I'd arrived, that I was big time. Of course, I was totally distraught when I lost it at summer camp and have never owned one since, but it still remained my greatest present.

Well, move the fuck over SpongeBob, you just got pwned.

This was now hands-down the most wonderful gift I'd ever received.

"It's an 18-carat white gold diamond. The jeweler said if I got it any bigger, your nostril would collapse," said Finch.

I flipped down the car visor to use the vanity mirror. I worked the old stud out, then carefully put the new one in. When I was done, I turned to Finch.

"How does it look?"

"Fantastic."

I pulled Finch toward me and gave him a deep, passionate kiss

designed to pitch a tent any Scoutmaster would've admired. I wanted
to do more, but then we really would've been late.

Fourteen

On the ride over, Finch could tell I was majorly stressing. I wasn't talking much, content mainly to chew on my cuticles. He finally reached over and took my hand.

"Relax," he said. "Leave some room for dinner."

I laughed and nodded. "Sorry."

"Everything's going to be fine. Hard part's over," Finch said.

"The hard part is getting through the next three hours."

"Look, a year ago, did you think any of this was even remotely possible?"

"Are you kidding?"

"Then it's all icing, right?"

He had a point. No matter what happened, and even if everybody hated my art, this was still a start. What I did with it after this night was up to me.

"Holy shit," marveled Finch.

"What?"

He nodded out the window as we passed by the gallery. There on the walls were my paintings, framed and ready to be judged by the world at large. Well, at least metropolitan Chicago. The caterers were inside setting up, with the opening still an hour away.

We parked across the street and walked to the gallery. Finch took my arm, something he'd never done before. It was both cute and very comforting, something I needed to calm my nervous butt down.

Once inside the gallery, I noticed it was a little warm. No matter, my jumpsuit was sleeveless and I'd made the right call by not wearing a blazer. Lenny was by the front desk going over last-minute details with Rosario, and when he saw me, flashed a big smile and came over to give me a hug.

"There's the main event," he said.

"Hi. Wow, everything looks great."

"Let's hope it all works out. AC is acting up a bit, but there's a maintenance man on the way over to fix it," Lenny assured me.

Finch was staring at a peculiar piece of sculpture that looked like a giant rock. I motioned to have him come join us.

"Lenny, this is Finch. He's a writer. Finch, this is Lenny, he owns the gallery."

Finch and Lenny shook hands.

"Nice to meet you," said Finch as he motioned to the sculpture. "Say, what is that?"

"Fuck if I know, but it sold two days ago for $1500."

"Interesting," Finch said.

Lenny picked up a clipboard. "It looks like we've got about eighty-five confirmed invites."

"Is that good or bad?" I said.

"Pretty good. Here's how it works. The first two hours are the press, invited guests, and gallery members, you give a little speech, and then the last hour we open it up to the general public."

"Speech?" I said, feeling myself go numb.

"Yeah, a little intro on yourself. Nothing fancy."

"Isn't that what the artist's statement is for?"

Lenny laughed. "Nobody reads that shit. They want to hear from the artist themselves."

He patted me on the back and walked into his office. How comforting it was to know that the intro I sweated every word over was going to be so summarily dismissed.

"Em, you've got this," Finch quietly said to me. "If a petrified turd can sell for $1500, you're not going to have any problem getting people to buy."

That was the least of my concerns right now. Knowing I'd have to give a speech had drained all the color from my face. I looked at Finch with my ashen expression. "Can I just pee on the ground now and get it over with?"

"What are you talking about?"

"Finch, I haven't done public speaking since fifth grade."

"Don't worry, you'll be fine."

No, I wouldn't be fine.

I was having flashbacks of me running on the Outsider Ticket trying to become fifth grade class president. Everyone had to give a speech, and I was up last. It went great for about the first three minutes, where I outlined the glorious vision I had for my elementary school. Some real utopian shit. Somehow, though, I got lost in my notes and started to stumble, which opened the floodgates for the verbal Molotovs to start flying. Naturally, I handled the catcalls with courage, dignity, and a healthy dose of pee running down my leg. I staggered through the rest of the speech, ending finally on a grace note of "Fuck y'all" before storming offstage. Not sure where the Southern inflection came from in my parting words, but it worked. It also earned me an express pass to the principal's office, a two-day suspension, and an immediate DQ from the election, which was just as well. I was way behind in the Quinnipiac Poll anyway.

With this late-breaking news about a speech hanging over me like a rusty guillotine blade, my stress level was now stratospheric. At least I had a little while before the horde descended. I knew I couldn't burn one or start drinking, that was just unprofessional, so I took refuge in pickles and shrimp from the food table. I burrowed away in a corner to make random notes on index cards about what to say.

Zero hour had finally arrived.

Finch and I stood near the back, and as the crowd filtered in, I could see they were definitely a "cocktail attire" group, with a few bohemian artist types thrown in the mix. I felt embarrassed that people were looking this classy, knowing what a slovenly mess everything was created in, but I guess Lenny had his dress code.

The place was filling in nicely, which also meant it was starting to get a little warmer with all the bodies now inside. Lenny walked to the front with a mic in his hand, and as I watched him, I tensed up. I knew I was up next.

"Hi, everyone, thanks for coming out tonight. The first order of business is I want to apologize for the temporary heat situation, we're working on it, but that's why we have a lovely bar in back. I don't want to take up too much time, I just want to introduce the artist who created all this interesting work you see. I initially met her a few months ago and like the obnoxious sort I am, I didn't pay her much attention. Weeks later when I finally saw her work and talked to her at length, I thought there was definitely something there. I hope you agree. If you do, make sure you let us know. Now, where is she?"

Finch nudged me, and I slowly raised my hand. Lenny motioned me to come forward.

"Emma Connolly, everyone."

There was courteous applause as I walked to the front, praying I wouldn't trip. As Lenny handed me the mic, all I could think about was to keep it clean. I was trying my best not to tremble as I faced a sea of total strangers.

"Hi," I said nervously.

That's it. I did it. May I leave?

Basking in my achievement of having uttered a greeting, I suddenly realized that I'd left the index cards in the back. I knew I'd look like an idiot if I went back to retrieve them, so here I was now having to wing it.

Mayday, mayday. We're going down. Brace for impact.

"I want to thank Lenny for allowing me the opportunity, and thanks to everyone for coming. This kind of shit...stuff, doesn't normally happen in my life."

Well, there goes the family audience.

As I was formulating what to say next, a thought struck me. It went back to that beach incident a few years ago where I almost drowned. What saved me then was I stopped struggling. Instead, I just relaxed and started to float. Now here I was trying not to drown again, and I realized the same concept might work.

"I've been painting since I was six, but I don't think my perspective has really changed all that much. I was drawn to the odd and random then, and still am now. I guess it shows an alarming lack of growth on my part."

This got a small laugh from the crowd. Hmm, maybe this wasn't so hard after all. Either that or they were an easy audience.

"There's this old joke, how many surrealists does it take to change a light bulb? The answer is a fish. The first time I heard that I think I was in high school and I remember laughing hysterically because it made absolutely no sense, which I guess explains why I like the style so much. Illogical just seemed kinda cool."

As I looked out over the faces, I noticed they were actually paying attention. Well, except for some jerkoff who'd been feverishly texting from the moment I started. Hey, Fingers, eyes up front. People are talking.

I was slowly gaining a little confidence the longer I stood up there because I was speaking about something I had a passion for, although flop sweat was never far behind. "I love how surrealism is like a dream. It comes out of those corners of your mind that you don't usually access. Well, at least not without some chemical assistance."

This got a couple of shout-outs from the group. All right, Em, pander to that 420 base.

"I can tell you that I absolutely loved creating these paintings, so I hope you like what you see. There's food in the back, and thank you again for coming, it really means a lot to me."

There was another small round of polite applause, I figured mainly because I was done. I was tempted to do a mic drop and say, "Em out, boyeee," but somehow I don't think it was the right crowd for that.

As I started to walk back, I felt a squeeze of my hand. I turned and Berri was behind me, looking at me with a proud mama's smile. She was dressed in a crop top, chartreuse mini-skirt, and white go-go boots, totally at odds with what most women were wearing. It was perfect.

"I enjoyed your speech. Very cogent and to the point."

I gave Berri a huge hug.

"Thanks. Should it have been longer?" I wondered.

"God no. You never want to be that artist who prattles on, boring everyone to tears."

"What do you think? Is this a decent turnout?"

"For your first time, I'd be very happy. It's always difficult to break new talent without a lot of hype. By the way, your paintings look lovely."

I was humbled. "Thanks. Berri, I just wanted to thank you for what you've done."

"Oh please," she said with a dismissive wave. "What has Berri done? Recommended you to someone? It's all on you now, darling. Let's just hope they're not here for the freebies and actually buy something."

"What am I supposed to do now?"

"Mingle. Press the flesh. Give people a face to associate with the work."

She could tell I was somewhat hesitant, but before I could offer any protest, she shooed me away. "Go, go. Create stories," she insisted.

I wandered back across the floor, meeting people and trying to hear any snippets of conversation. I picked up on "It's either buy this or pay for my hair transplants," "How do you think this would look in the restroom?" and "I thought I had problems." None were real ringing endorsements, but I knew my work would never be everyone's cup of poison.

As I walked back to where Finch was, I noticed Tomas, the writer from the *Sentinel*, was off to the side involved in a conversation with a trio of people. He saw me and gave a quick thumbs-up, which really felt good.

"Okay, how was I?" I asked Finch, wanting the unvarnished truth.

"Greatest speech ever, and you didn't say 'fuck' once," he said.

"A personal best. I didn't sound too pretentious?"

"Along with demure, that's probably the last word I'd ever associate with you."

The back door to the gallery opened and Bolan swept in with Sheridan in tow. The two of them looked like they'd come straight off New York Fashion Week, which now made me really start to second-guess my outfit. I began to feel like I'd gotten dressed at a military surplus store.

"I told you it'd be open," Bolan said to Sheridan.

He was carrying a foil-wrapped plate, and as soon as Bolan saw me, I waved him over.

"Hey, Superstar," Bolan said to me.

"Why are you guys coming in that way? Your name is on the list."

"Valet was taking forever, so I just parked in the back. Besides, it's a much more stylish entrance this way."

Bolan gave me a kiss on the cheek and handed me the plate.

"I said that you didn't have to bring anything. It's being catered," I objected.

"I always come bearing gifts."

Bolan shook Finch's hand and put his arm around his shoulder. "And there's the poet laureate. Man, I can't thank you enough for what you wrote. People who know me says it actually makes me sound human."

Finch laughed. "Glad to help. Everyone I've talked to is dying to know who the article is about. Oh, and you've got two standing marriage proposals from it."

Bolan smiled at Sheridan and rubbed her back. "Yeah, I'm good."

I set Bolan's plate on the catering table, then noticed that Sheridan was being her usual quiet self. Oh my God, stop! She was staring at me with those insane crystalline blue eyes again. She was like Medusa in reverse, stare at her eyes and you were reduced to a puddle instead of stone. All I could do was gawk at her like some moony teenager.

"Hi," I said to Sheridan.

She looked like she was ready to burst unless she said something, then finally rushed toward me and wrapped her arms around my neck in a fierce hug. I didn't know quite how to react, as I saw Bolan shake his head.

"Sher, you're strangling her," he said.

Sheridan pulled back, eyes brimming with tears. I had no earthly idea what was going on with her. I didn't know I had this effect on people.

"Do you know how long I've been wanting to do that?" Sheridan asked me.

"Not really, no," I said.

"Remember when we met at that party?"

I nodded but remained confused.

"And you said I should stop making excuses and take art classes?"

"Well, that's not quite what I said, but..."

"You were right. And I have been, and I absolutely love it. It's changed my whole life."

"Yeah, thanks, Em. She won't stop drawing me," Bolan chimed in.

I was delighted. "Oh my God, that's great. What type of classes?"

"Life drawing, basic oil painting, I'm even taking an art history class now on weekends," she said, bubbling over with excitement. I mean, the girl was turnt.

She continued to gush until Bolan was finally able to get a word in.

"Time out. Okay, so who's drinking what?" Bolan asked.

"Can you just get me some water, please?" I said.

"Red vino works for me," Finch added.

"Just get me whatever," Sheridan said.

"I'm on it," Bolan said.

She turned her attention back to me. "And the best thing about it is..."

"Sher, can you help me, please? I've only got two hands," said Bolan.

As Sheridan walked away with Bolan, she looked back at me and mouthed "Thank you" while I smiled, feeling thrilled I'd had a positive impact on someone's life.

"You're not going to believe this," said Finch.

"What?"

"Follow me."

As I walked with Finch across the gallery, I was stopped by an older couple in their seventies. The man had that leathery type of tan, with a full head of silver hair that looked like a lion's mane. He pointed at the program, then at me.

"Pardon, you're the *pittrice*?" he said in a thick Italian accent.

"I'm sorry?"

"The painter," he clarified.

"Yes, I am."

"Ah, *bene*. Forgive, my English not so good. I want to say my wife and I like your exhibition very much."

"Thank you. I'm sorry for the conditions."

"What? Oh, you mean hot," he laughed. "I'm from Bergamo. This is nothing. Do you have a business card?"

"All my information is in the program."

He flipped through the program and nodded. "Ah, *si si*. Thank you. My name is Ruggero. This is my wife, Luciana."

His wife was an elegant woman who looked like she could've come off a Botticelli painting.

"Lovely work," she said.

"Well, I just say thanks again. I enjoy very much," he added.

"Thank you for coming."

As they blended back into the crowd, Finch winked at me. "See, you're already an international sensation."

We continued walking up to the front, where I got my first shock of the young evening. There was Grieg taking in the exhibition. He was intensely studying the paintings as Finch approached him.

"Grieg, hi," said Finch.

Grieg looked over at Finch. "Hello. Do I know you?"

"We took one of your drawing classes together," Finch said, motioning to the two of us.

"Ah, I see."

"Do you remember us?"

"I'm sorry, I have so many students."

"What do you think of the paintings?" I asked.

Grieg let out what I could only really term as an exhaustive sigh.

"Well, thank you for coming out to my exhibition, anyway," I said, smiling through gritted teeth.

"*You're* the artist here?" Grieg asked.

"Yes, I am," I said.

Grieg just nodded, then smiled at me. "Well, congratulations."

"Thanks."

"Perhaps you should've taken a few more of my classes, no?"

He walked away, but somehow I just couldn't be mad. There was something admirable about his unfailing assholiness.

I surveyed the crowd and saw that more people were talking with each other than looking at the paintings. That bugged me, because although I knew it was a social gathering and all, to me it was like people who kept checking their cell phones during a concert. Just rude. I noticed a short girl with red hair and a cocktail glass in one hand was taking a ton of selfies in front of the paintings, which I guess meant she liked what she saw. At least she was paying attention.

The text alert on my phone went off. I had a message that read "Let an emo girl in already!" I heard a tapping on the front glass and glanced up to see Natalie standing outside.

No. Fucking. Way.

I screamed, then sheepishly looked around because of my outburst. I motioned her to come to the front door.

"Be right back," I said to Finch.

I walked over to the guy with the guest list on a tablet. "Please let her in," I said, pointing to Natalie.

"She's not on the list," he replied.

"I know, but she's with me."

"And who are you?"

I grabbed a program and handed it to him with the back cover face up with my picture on it. He waved inside Natalie, who gave him a smirk as she passed.

"Told you I don't do lists," she said to him.

Once inside, Natalie nearly knocked me over with her embrace. I struggled to keep my balance.

"You came," I gasped.

"Fuck yeah, I came. Why wouldn't I?"

"Because you said you couldn't."

"C'mon, Em, you should know by now never listen to me."

I realized we were blocking the entrance, so I motioned Natalie over to where Finch was standing.

"But the last email I got from you said you couldn't make it," I said.

"That was before I threatened my husband with sexual embargoes. I told him I wasn't going to miss the biggest night for my BFF from Bellamy."

"God, Natalie, this means so much to me. Thank you for coming. Oh here, I've got to introduce you. Finch, this is Natalie, my touchstone from high school, and Nat, this is Finch, the coolest person on the planet."

"Hello, 'coolest person on the planet,'" Natalie said as she shook hands with Finch.

"Hi, great to meet you. Exactly what kind of sexual embargoes are we talking about?"

I dropped my head in embarrassment. "Awkward."

Natalie smiled and pointed a finger at Finch. "Oh, I like you." She glanced around the gallery, then at me. "Yo, what's up with the heat? This is like Miami miserable."

"Don't ask." I shook my head, then motioned for her to follow me. "C'mon. We'll get the illusion it's cooler if we're moving."

Along with Finch, I took Natalie on a guided tour of my paintings. She was totally blown away by them. She was always honest to a fault, so if she didn't like something, she would've said so. Natalie always used to tell me I looked like a Russian mail-order bride in my yearbook photos, which I probably did. What girl doesn't?

After we got through with the last painting, Natalie turned to me. "Em, this shit is berserk. I knew you had talent, but this is like fucked-for-life talent."

"Thanks," I said.

She slapped Finch on the shoulder. "Dude, don't let her get away. You won't do better."

As the three of us stood talking in the middle of the gallery, the red-haired girl who had been busy taking selfies earlier came over to me. She was at Defcon 1 on the inebriated scale.

"Can you do me a favor? Can I get a picture with you and...." she said, then stopped. She did a staggered pirouette around the gallery, then realized the painting she wanted to pose with was directly behind her.

"Thatone!" she slurred and pointed.

This was surely going to be a test of my will. Not only did I despise selfies, I also hated sloppy drunks, but wanting to be a good sport, I reluctantly agreed. Drunk Gurl tried to hand Natalie her full cocktail glass.

"Fuck off. Hire a maid," Natalie snapped.

"Mean," said Drunk Gurl, who frowned at Natalie.

She decided to chug the drink instead, then motioned me to come join her in front of the painting. It's always advisable to never selfie while hammered, as she couldn't get a picture she liked. Finally, I agreed to take the shot until she got one she was happy with. I handed her the phone back, and she admiringly looked down at the picture.

"Thanks," she said. "Your stuff is freakin' brilliant."

Then without as much as even a warm-up burp, Drunk Gurl proceeded to hurl all over her phone. This was immediately followed by that inevitable moment of silence where no one quite believes what's happened.

"I just bought this!" she wailed, looking at her puke-encrusted phone.

Sorry for your loss. No, I'm not.

She started sobbing as people began to give us wide berth.

Meanwhile, here's the thing about airborne vomit. It needs a place to land, and that it did, raining down on my open-toed shoes. I quickly stepped back, hoping to avoid any after-dribble, but it didn't matter. I could already feel the chunky liquid wedging in between my toes.

Believe it or not, my first impulse was to hold Natalie back. I knew she would go after Drunk Gurl and considering she was almost a foot taller than her, it could get real ugly fast. In eleventh grade, Natalie had ripped out the earring of a girl who had stolen a pair of sunglasses from me. Yanked straight out, torn lobe and everything. I think she kept the earring as a trophy.

"Stupid drunk bitch," Natalie snarled as she stepped toward her. I hurriedly got between the two to stop any uprising.

"Nat, it's fine. Don't worry about it."

Natalie backed off as Drunk Gurl weaved her way outside to properly mourn the death of her device.

Meanwhile, I went to the restroom to clean off the spew. While I was in there doing the best to save my Cole Haans, a couple of girls about my age came in to gossip and reapply their already overdone makeup. Their main topic of conversation was about what galleries offered the best open bars and free feeds. I was amazed at their meticulous detailing of how to make an evening of gallery hopping into an epicurean event. They ended by comparing food they'd stashed in their purses, offering glowing reviews of their hauls, especially the cookies, which one of the girls said she was starting to get a little buzz from.

This got my attention. I walked over to them and asked where they got the cookies from. They said they were on a plate out on the table, and I immediately grabbed my shoes and bolted from the restroom.

I made a beeline for the catering table. I looked at the plate Bolan had brought in, which was now half empty. I inspected the cookies, taking a bite out of one. It tasted like regular chocolate chip, but that's not how CBD edibles work. You've got to give them time to deliver their magic.

I went on a hunt for Bolan and found him canoodling with Sheridan in a corner of the gallery.

"Bolan, you brought the cookies in," I said in an accusatory tone.

"Yeah, why?" he said.

"What's in them?"

"Just a little something something," Bolan grinned.

I was furious with him. "Are you nuts? You can't bring that shit to a place like this."

"Relax. There's barely enough in there to get a fly high. Besides, I think it'll help people appreciate your paintings more."

"Oh my God," I said, now in full freak-out mode. I turned and walked back over to the catering table, where a woman was just picking up a cookie off the plate. I yanked it out of her hand.

"Excuse me," she said, quite indignant.

"Sorry, but this fell on the ground earlier. Totally violated the five-second rule. Try the strawberry cheesecake. Killer."

She took my advice as I grabbed Bolan's plate and stashed it under the table. The crisis was somewhat averted, although as I looked out over the crowd, I could see at least four people were still eating the cookies. Well, weren't they in for a fucking surprise.

As the evening wore on, I hung mostly with Natalie and Finch, as I was pretty much a stress mess. The general public had been let in, and now the place was really crowded and *really* hot, with people fanning themselves like we were in the Deep South. I finally decided to go ask Lenny if there was anything he could do about getting the place under Sudan-level temperatures. I found him standing outside by the entrance, smoking a cigarette. Yeah, of course, he didn't want to be inside sweating his balls off.

"Hi, I was just checking to see if there's any word on fixing the air?"

"The guy's running late on another call, but he promised he'd be here."

I checked my watch. It was after 9 p.m. "Do they even come this late?"

"They do when I'm going to pay them overtime. Don't worry, this has happened before. Doesn't mean a thing. This is a Chicago crowd. They'll sit out at Wrigley in 100-degree weather and not care."

Yes, except that's open-air, with a wind, and they're usually ten beers down. A nuclear bomb could drop and they'd think it was fireworks.

To say I was grievously unhappy at Lenny's blasé attitude would be a grotesque understatement, but what could I do? I walked back inside, all kinds of peeved.

On the way back to join Finch and Natalie, I passed a man who was staring inches away from one of the paintings and giggling uncontrollably. Evidently, someone was enjoying his cookie.

I stood in back bitching about the circumstances, until the sound of a woman's scream silenced everyone. Up near the front, a heavyset man had collapsed on the floor. Fifteen minutes later a team of paramedics were wheeling him out. The man's wife was arguing with Lenny that the room temperature had contributed to what'd happened to her husband. I smelled a lawsuit.

This was welcome news to Bolan, who feared someone had had a bad reaction to his chocolate chip creations. Once in the clear, Bolan apologized to me, wished me luck, and took off into the night with Sheridan. They were the lucky ones, while I had to endure until the bitter end, which came when there were about four people left. I checked with Lenny, and there had not been a single sale. Gee, what a shock, and under such optimal conditions.

The evening had been, for all intents and purposes, a total bust.

Natalie, Finch, and I all went outside to the back alley, where we sat and ate the rest of Bolan's cookies. Anything to alleviate the sting of defeat.

Finch tried to put a positive spin on things. "I don't know, until the guy got the massive heart attack, I think things were going okay."

Natalie and I gave him a look. "Just sayin'," he offered.

"Em, it doesn't matter what happened tonight. What matters is you did this. No one can ever take that away from you," enthused Natalie. "Okay, I just turned into you ten years ago. That's horrifying."

I was on my third cookie when a van pulled up and parked near us. Guess fucking who? The AC guy had finally arrived. He got out and glanced around at the group of unmarked back doors he had to choose from.

"Do you guys know which entrance is Czymanek Gallery?"

"Yeah, it's the fourth one to the left," motioned Natalie.

"Thanks," he said, wandering off with toolbox in hand.

"No problem," said Natalie. She slapped Finch on the back. "Go get a knife. His tires are toast."

After a couple of minutes, the repairman came back accompanied by a busboy who pointed him to the right door. The repairman walked by us and gave Natalie a hateful look.

"Oops, my bad. Sowwy," she called after him.

As Natalie and Finch continued their best to try and console me, I just remained quiet, which was always a sure sign I was down. Finally, after about fifteen minutes of barely saying a word, I spoke up.

"I want to get inked," I emphatically stated.

We found a tattoo parlor open late in Greektown, and I sat down to go under the needle one more time. The tat would be joining my other two small ones: a four-leaf clover on my ankle and a blue flamingo I had done on my shoulder blade. I got the clover on my 21st birthday for obvious lineage reasons, and the blue flamingo was because I'd loved them since reading about them as a kid, and always felt a connection because their eyes could change color.

This time I was getting a small paintbrush with sparks shooting off the tip, to be drawn on the inside of my right forefinger. Why? Because I wanted something to always remind me of the evening.

I encouraged Natalie to take the bodyworks plunge, but she was content to sit and be enthralled watching the art come to life, while Finch took the occasion to add another piercing to his gallery of metal.

Once finished, we hunkered down at an all-night diner to eat until about 3 a.m., then crashed back at my place. Five hours later I was up to take Natalie to the airport, while Finch slept in.

As we sat curbside in the loading zone, Natalie refused to let me get morose about the opening. The surprising thing is she did it with a minimal amount of threats.

"Listen, Em, fuck last night. You've still got two weeks on display in that gallery."

"Which isn't a guarantee of anything," I said.

"It means you're going to be seen. You just have to keep at this shit."

I nodded. "You're right."

"I always am. Look, I sell furniture for a living. Of course, I'm fabulously successful at it, but you create. Everyone has to use their minds with what you do, while people park their wrinkly asses on what I do."

"Thanks for the visual."

"It's true. Dude, you've got mad skillz. You're my fucking hero and always have been. Now give me a hug, I gotta go."

I didn't want to let go of her as we embraced. "I'll let you know what happens. And Natalie, thanks again for coming here," I said.

"Just don't make me regret it."

As Natalie got out, she looked at the parking officer who had his pad out and was poised to write me up for loitering in the white zone. "Hey, don't ticket her. I'm handicapped," she barked.

"You look fine to me."

"Oh yeah? You sexually harass all the female customers?"

He shook his head and closed his book. I waved goodbye to Natalie and took off before the officer changed his mind.

Fifteen

For the next week I kept checking the *Sentinel* to see if I even warranted a mention. A review eventually popped up on Saturday, the least-read day of the week. A tiny, one-paragraph review that one might've mistaken for your average obituary.

Which it was.

It featured such hosannas as "derivative," "befuddling," and "bereft of merit," and ended with the glowing, "Rarely has provocation seemed so perfunctory." So, outside of a few nitpicks, Tomas basically dug it? Ironically, it didn't bother me as much as I thought it would. Sure, I would've liked to have had roses tossed at my feet, who wouldn't, but I had done this for me and no one else. The only annoying part was Tomas had been such a weasel about it. You don't give someone a thumbs up, only to trash them later. You say it to them at the event. "Your art sucks, you have no talent, but the food's great!"

I haunted the gallery for the next two weeks, but always from a distance. I would cruise by on my lunch break or after work to see if anyone was in there checking things out, yet I never went inside.

Dropping in to constantly ask how things were going struck me as way too needy and/or borderline stalking. There were always people in there, ranging from a couple to about a dozen depending on what time of day, so at least that was encouraging.

When the two weeks were over, I got a call from Rosario asking me to come in and collect my work. I walked into the gallery and could see the paintings were boxed and ready to go. The new exhibit, a series of oil paintings of nothing but multi-colored doors, inexplicably called "*The Doors*," had taken my place. Three of the paintings already had "sold" snipes on the corners.

"So, what was the final tally?" I asked Rosario.

"Well, you did sell a couple," she said as she thumbed through the invoices.

"No way!" I was pumped. Here I was expecting abject failure, although I wasn't sure how happy Lenny was going to be selling two paintings in two weeks. His cut probably didn't even cover the bar tab for the opening.

I pretty much got my answer when I glanced in his office and saw him on the phone. I waved to him as he looked straight at me. He continued the call and turned his chair away without the slightest acknowledgment. Fucking cold-blooded, I thought.

"Let me go see about your check," Rosario said.

She walked into Lenny's office, and as she did so, I snuck a peek at the invoices for the two sales. My heart sank. One purchase was by Bolan, and the other invoice I saw was for the name Farmer in Miami. Unless there was the most incredible coincidence, which there wasn't, Natalie had bought the other painting. That meant outside of immediate friends, I sold nothing.

Zip. Nada. Nil.

Rosario came out of the office, an apologetic look on her face. "Hi, Lenny says we'll cut the check at the end of the month when we pay all the other invoicing."

I packed up my paintings and left, wondering if this was really how they paid artists or just my punishment for paltry sales.

I was tempted to call and thank Natalie for buying something, but the fact she never mentioned it made me think she didn't want me to know. When I went over to Bolan's place for provisions, the painting he bought was nowhere to be found. Maybe he'd given it to Sheridan for safekeeping, or it was locked away in some attic with a batshit uncle, I don't know, but it was the same deal with him too, not a single word about it.

This almost made me feel like a charity case. Fuck almost. It did.

The whole thing had been a learning experience, but I ain't gonna lie. It threw me into a bit of a depression. When you put everything of yourself into something, only to be met with virtual indifference, it tends to cast a shroud over your life.

Knowing I still had possibilities to get people to see my work, I kept the website going, although I did have the comments disabled. Lots of lonely, stupid people out there.

My next plan of attack was to hit up an art fair. There were higher-end fairs, but those cost a small fortune to display at, so I settled for the more cost-effective one. The kind that basically resembled a swap meet for artists. You sat in a small tent all day and roasted your ass off while a collection of lookie-loos came by asking vapid questions and tried to buy your work for a tenth of what you were asking. Okay, to be fair, that's a gross generalization, but I feel comfortable with it. I had to hold court for eight hours, fighting both a wind that threatened to buckle the tent, and creepy older guys, who'd strike up convos with no intent to buy. I did sell a painting for $75 to a broke college couple who looked like they were living off ramen, making my total net profit on the day, after expenses, a whopping -$325.

This was how kingdoms were built.

I don't know how people did these things without going insane, but I was clearly not cut out for this style of business.

Where did all this leave me? Right back where I started. The emotional roller-coaster of inactivity followed by creative surges had once again ground to a halt, only now it was edging toward derailment. I'd stopped painting again, finding no inspiration to pick up the brush. In short, my old bad habits were seeping back into my life and foolishly I welcomed them like some long-lost friends. Through it all, Finch was the best about my current state of malaise, loving when I needed it and kicking my butt when I needed it more.

At work, I continued to cement my status as one of the janitorial supply industry's brightest stars, finally winning the vaunted title of "Associate of the Month," which I thought I was in the running for a few months back. Talk about overdue honors. I wound up getting my name on a plaque and a free lunch. Who needs artistic approval when you can score props like that?

I had a 4 p.m. appointment in South Loop to close the deal on supplying a chain of health clubs, and barely made it on time. After circling the block, I was able to wedge myself in between two large box trucks. Such was the beauty of Minis. I hurried inside and for the next thirty minutes gave my best pitch to the owner, who sounded like he was one step away from needing an oxygen tent. His hacking, wheezing, and coughing provided a respiratory underscore to my pitch. I wasn't sure if he saw the irony of a health club owner sounding like he had black lung, but it didn't matter. At the end of it all, he said yes.

I called Hendu to let him know the good news and walked out pleased I could add another notch to my sales bedpost.

My elation lasted all of about two minutes.

It's quite the feeling when you come out to find an empty street. It literally takes your breath away, until you realize you'll need it to scream at the world. In my haste to make the appointment and thanks to the big-ass truck in front of me, I never saw the street sign forbidding parking from 4–6 p.m., and now some tow-truck driver had come and taken my Mini to car prison.

Nearly two hours later, I was finally able to reclaim my precious at the tow yard, leaving me $150 lighter and completely dispirited. By the time I got home, I wanted nothing more than to crawl into a fetal position and return to the womb. Who am I kidding? My mother wouldn't have me.

I dragged through the building complex, stopping off to get the mail. Bills, junk flyers, ooh, M Burger coupons, more bills, and an envelope addressed to me in handwriting. I looked at it quizzically, then opened it and within moments of reading the contents slid to the ground, putting my hand over my mouth in complete astonishment.

I don't even recall how long it took me to drive over to Finch's place, but I probably broke a few basic traffic laws along the way. As I rode the ramshackle elevator up to his loft, I was a tightly wrapped bundle of nervous energy ready to explode. I got off the elevator and walked to the door, where I could hear yelling going on inside. I knocked and got no response. I knocked harder with the same result, then followed up with the always popular fist-pounding. Still nothing, just primal screams coming from the loft. I finally took out my phone and furiously texted Finch. A few moments later he opened the door.

"Hi, sorry, I didn't hear you knock. We're pulling a *COD* all-nighter. What's up? What couldn't you tell me on the phone?"

He could see my excitement level was on overload as I slightly bounced up and down.

"Jesus, what is it? You look like you need Ritalin. Is everything okay?" he asked.

Hollers from inside demanded his return, but I grabbed him by the arm, pulling him out into the hallway.

"Do you remember that little Italian man I met at the opening?" I said.

"Not really."

"The guy who was with his wife. After he left, you said I was on my way to becoming an international sensation."

Finch searched his memory. "Right, right. What about him?"

"Well, it turns out that little guy is actually a pretty big guy."

"How? What do you mean?"

I pulled out the letter I received and handed it to Finch. He started reading it and shook his head. "Oh wow."

"I know, isn't it incredible?" I gushed.

"No, I mean there's some really bad syntax and punctuation here," he said, the writer in him taking over.

I grabbed the letter back. "Then I'll tell you what it says. Turns out that guy and his wife run an art institute in Italy and come over here periodically to scout out artists. Anyway, they liked my work so much, they invited me for a residency in Bergamo, painting, studying, hanging out with other artists, whatever I want to do."

Finch's eyes opened wide and he let out a yell. "Em, that's fucking incredible!"

"All I have to do is pay for the flight, they'll take care of the rest."

He furrowed his brow. "Wait, there's not like a Nigerian prince involved, is there?"

I gave Finch a withering look.

"Just want to make sure. That's unreal. How long would you be gone for?" he asked.

"Six months."

Those two words took Finch totally off guard, and he ever so slightly recoiled. "Six months? Long time. What about your job? What about your place?"

"I don't know yet. I'm still trying to wrap my head around this."

"Holy shit, six months," Finch repeated, his voice dropping. I don't know if he was even trying to hide it, but I could sense he was feeling deflated.

I grabbed his hands and pulled him close. I gave him an impassioned look.

"No, no, no. Don't go there. Please. Finch, except for you, I've pretty much made almost a decade of bad to terrible choices that've gotten me where I am. Fucking stuck in amber like those bugs they sell at the Field. I just get the feeling that if I don't do this, if I don't blow up my life now, another ten years will go by and I'll still have some shitty job, be living in some crappy apartment, smoking weed and gaming. Finch, I know me. And I know I need to scare myself."

"Well, are you definitely going?"

"I'm still kind of cooking this up in my brain, but everything keeps leading to the same answer."

"Which is?"

"Yes. When would I ever get this chance again? Why, you don't think I should go?"

"Of course you should go. It's just that...I don't know. Fuck, I was just really starting to like you."

I smiled. "It's not like I'd be moving there forever."

As he leaned back against the wall and stared at me, I could tell he was sad.

"Who knows? You could meet some swarthy Italian guy, fall in love, and retire to a villa on Lake Como. It does happen."

I didn't know if he was kidding. I assumed he was. This was the first time I'd ever seen Finch display anything close to hurt, unless you counted the time he impaled himself on the palette knife.

"Not happening," I said.

"If you go, I have to embrace all scenarios."

"Fair enough," I said.

There were a couple of awkward moments of silence where neither one of us knew what to say. It was so unlike us.

I finally took the initiative and walked up close to him, searching his eyes for an understanding. "Finch, someone finally gets what I want to do. That means everything to me. Goals, right?"

After a moment, he let out a small smile and nodded.

I knew I faced a real problem. Take the offer and inflict unspeakable sorrow on a person I cared deeply about, or don't go and probably regret the decision forever. (A slight lean toward the overdramatic here. It heightens reality.) The bottom line was I'd grown stale in Chicago. It wasn't the city's fault, it was mine. The place rocked, but for twenty-seven years it was all I'd known. The U.S. Census said that 70 percent of Midwesterners still lived in the state they were born in, and that half of the adults there never left their hometown. Jesus, I'd become a stat, and not a good one at that.

So here I was again, staring down that old frenemy of mine: opportunity. Whatever I chose, I knew I'd bounce the decision around a thousand times, like some roulette ball from Hell. One day it'd be all systems go, the next I'd want to melt back into the creature comforts of home. Stagnation is a tough fucking nut to break. Maybe the toughest.

My ultimate decision began somewhere on the Stevenson Expressway at about 6 p.m., a few days after I got the letter. While I agonizingly crawled through single-digit speeds on the road, I glanced around at the other drivers in adjoining cars. Everyone looked like they were on their way to a funeral.

Their own.

A vision began to form in my mind of a gridlocked freeway with the drivers floating free from their cars, blissfully headed to whereabouts unknown. The name *"Auto Salvation"* immediately popped into my head.

With the idea still freshly imprinted in my brain, I got home, made up a canvas, and started work on it. Two days later, the painting was complete. As I stood there looking at it, I had the answer to my dilemma right in front of me and didn't even realize it. Talk about freaky and unintentional, but one of the figures I painted floating from their car looked a lot like me.

Swear to Christ, I never even thought of that while I was creating it, I just needed bodies, all genders, shapes, and sizes. Yet somehow my subconscious had bubbled to the surface, telling me what I needed to do, and I always listened to my subconscious. For me, it was the only thing that provided clarity.

I was going.

Some major decisions needed to be made. What to do with my apartment was first. My lease agreement didn't allow me to sublet and paying rent for six months on an empty place made no sense, so I gave my thirty-day notice. Just like that. After five years there, I was giving up my cozy little hovel, and when I did, I knew that shit was about to get real.

Next in line was my job. I told Hendu about my plan and he immediately offered to increase my salary. When I said it wasn't about the money, he became convinced some rival company was trying to poach me. I reassured him it was nothing but a personal choice, a concept he was having trouble accepting, but after hearing me speak passionately about what I was going to do, he gave me his blessing. He said I could stay on until I was ready to leave, and that I'd always have a place if I ever wanted my old job back. Who knew I'd find such a warm and loving home in the world of toilet supplies?

Between the money I was earning, money I had saved, and what I made selling off things like furniture, jewelry, and my body (joking), I figured I'd be able to bank about $6K. I'd always been good with money, but now it'd really be put to the test. Housing was being provided, so as long as I didn't turn into some gluttonous sow and OD on Italian food and wine, I probably would be okay.

With the big-ticket items of my job and apartment out of the way, it was now time to start working on the smaller details of my escape, like getting a passport and visa. My flight wasn't for a few weeks, but I still got the travel stuff expedited. This is going to sound totally provincial, but I'd never owned a passport in my life. Never had any need to. When it arrived, I sent Natalie a picture of my passport photo with the caption "Russian mail-order bride ready to jet."

I rented more space at the storage facility, which would now house the rest of my life. The time had come to blow up the clutter, and holy fuck, did I have a lot of it. I filled up one of those large communal trash bins with my stuff, something I'm sure the other tenants weren't thrilled about. As things started to disappear from my apartment, the place kept getting bigger and bigger. Hey, where did that wall come from?

Finch was going to keep my paintings in case any of them sold, and just as important, I was leaving him with my Mini. This was the ultimate sign of trust. He had an extra parking place at his building, so there it would sit awaiting my return. He was under strict orders he had to run it once a week, wash it once a month, and keep it covered. And under no condition could he fuck with my Sirius presets, which would be an act beyond betrayal.

As the clock ticked down on my departure, I started to have second thoughts. What if I hated where I was going? Was the language barrier going to be a nightmare? What if I got homesick? I entertained these and other possibilities until I ultimately realized none of it mattered. I had made my choice and was going to see it through.

Total commitment. A new me, or an old me, just rejuiced.

My last night in the apartment was sort of a melancholy thing. I told you I got weird about places. This was my home, only now it wasn't. Now it was a shell for someone else to inhabit, just like some hermit crab. Everything was gone except for my couch, a chest of drawers, a rack of clothes, the TV, and the bed.

Finch came over and brought dinner. We could've gone out and had a big farewell party somewhere, but all I really wanted to do was spend my last night in Chicago just kicking back with him. We smoked my last bit of Cinderella 99 in a toast to my apartment and new beginnings. I know I certainly wasn't the same person leaving there that I was when I arrived.

And we fucked.

Once.

It was well below our usual Olympian marathon sessions, but the way I figured, that one time would stand out a lot more. Something to deposit in the memory bank and accrue prurient interest on over the next half year.

I was booked on an evening flight, so I slept in until noon. Finch had gone to rent a truck and bring back a roommate to help him move the remaining big stuff. Final jury deliberations began over packing (and unpacking) the clothes I was going to take with me. Once I had decided on what made the cut, I dragged my bulging suitcases into the living room. I knew I was going to get slaughtered on weight charges, but what was the alternative? Better to have too many choices than not enough. I just hoped it wouldn't drag the plane down.

I walked back down the hallway to get my equally overstuffed carry-on. At least I wouldn't get clipped on that.

"I hoped you've packed warmly. You have no idea how brutal Italian winters can be."

I stopped dead in my tracks at the familiar voice. I slowly walked back into the living room, where Mr. Spangler was looking out the balcony window.

"You're telling someone from Chicago about winter?" I said.

He turned and looked at me. "Excellent argument."

Mr. Spangler proceeded to walk around the empty apartment, nodding approvingly. "I love what you've done with the place."

"Funny," I said. "I thought you left for good."

"That was the original plan, but I felt compelled to come back and congratulate you on all your success. Your own exhibition. Very impressive."

"Yeah, that was real epic," I scoffed.

"All that matters is the end result. A residency."

I was surprised, even though I knew I shouldn't have been. "How do you even know about this stuff?"

"The other side is very resourceful. Much better than the internet, and without all that annoying spam."

I sat down on the couch, trying to think of the best way to say what needed to be said, but struggling with it. I always fumbled when it came to gratitude.

"I'm thinking a 'thank you' seems kind of pitifully inadequate at this point. I wouldn't have done any of this without you," I said.

"Oh, I think eventually you would have. True talent has a way of not leaving one alone, as I'm sure you've now discovered."

"Well, thank you for helping, but mostly, thank you for caring," I said, trying not to sound too choked up, but failing.

"Miss Connolly, it's been my pleasure."

"So now what?" I asked.

"Well, like you said, I can 'move on.'"

"To where?"

"To a much higher plane of existence," he said solemnly.

"Really?"

Mr. Spangler cackled and doubled over. "I'm sorry. I can't say that with a straight face. If you only knew what absolute horseshit all that is. Actually, I'm headed down to the Azores. I got stuck with a timeshare I never got to use, so I'm going to get my money's worth. So to speak.

"Cool," I said. "Wait, so what you're telling me is none of it is true?"

"None of what?"

"This whole 'higher plane' thing."

He looked at me with an enigmatic smile. "I'll let you decide that for yourself many, many years from now."

He walked over to the now legendary living room closet.

"Really? You're going to do the whole closet thing again?" I said.

Mr. Spangler shrugged. "It works."

I smiled. "I guess it does."

He opened the door and stared back at me. "I do want to wish you good luck, though."

"Luck is for amateurs. Wish me success," I said, stealing from a noted teacher.

He grinned at having seen his words taken root. "I do wish you success. And happiness. Always."

I was about to totally lose it as my eyes welled with tears. I put up a hand. "Okay, that's it. You gotta go. Please. I have a plane to catch and I can't be an emotional wreck. I'm saving that for the airport."

"Will do." He waved and stepped inside the closet, closing the door for the last time.

After a few moments, I got up and walked over to the closet. I reached down to open it, then thought better and just let it be.

From inside, I heard his voice say, "Goodbye, Emma."

I leaned my head gently against the door. "Goodbye, Mr. Spangler."

Finch and I stood in the middle of a packed O'Hare Airport staring at the huge arrival and departure board. I finally found my flight and groaned.

"Great, flight's been delayed."

"Uh oh, maybe it's all a sign," Finch said. "You want to get something to eat?"

"I'm too nervous to eat."

"Why?"

"It's a ten-hour flight."

"So?"

"Finch, I've never been on a plane for longer than two hours. Plus, I've never flown over water before, let alone left the U.S."

Finch put both his hands on my shoulders. "My advice to you. Those mini liquor bottles they sell? Say yes to everything. You've got your passport?"

A look of sheer terror crossed my face. "Oh my God!" I exclaimed.

"Em, please tell me you didn't forget it."

I slowly raised my arm, waving my brand-new passport and grinning like a fiend.

"Virgin paper," I bragged.

Finch took it out of my hand and looked at it. "This says you're thirty-five."

I snatched it back to check. The birth date was fine. "Maybe I'll stay longer," I said, narrowing my eyes. "So, what are you going with your new-found freedom?"

"Write my ass off. You've inspired me. Hey, that reminds me, in all the excitement, I forgot to tell you. I've picked up a little heat off the Bolan article. I was contacted by a couple of alt-weeklies and online sites to ask if I wanted to write for them," Finch said.

I shoved Finch, annoyed at this late-breaking news. "What is wrong with you? You're supposed to tell me this shit *when* it happens. Not as an afterthought."

"No way, this is your time now. Besides, I don't know, it still doesn't really make me a 'writer' writer, but at least this way I can annoy the city in a much more ubiquitous manner."

"Well, congrats. That's great. Send me everything."

Finch looked at me. "Let me ask you something. You would've gone regardless of what I said, right?"

I nodded.

"Good," he smiled. "And I want to apologize for acting all butthurt when you first told me."

"Why? I would've worried if you hadn't."

"Although it's still a really long time," Finch said. "Promise me you'll Skype every day?"

I hesitated. "Finch, I don't know what my schedule..."

"I'm joking. Don't you dare," he said. "Make me miss you."

"You better, because I'll sure as fuck miss you."

I dropped my carry-on bag and hugged him.

Tight. And then tighter.

People pushed by us, but I didn't care. I was not about to move an inch or let go, no matter what. I was also trying not to break down but wound up shaking as a result of my stupid defiance. I buried my face in his chest.

"God, I've got all the fucking feels now. I don't know whether to cry or laugh or be freaked or what," I said.

"Just be safe," Finch whispered in my ear.

Finch and I said our tearful goodbyes at TSA check-in, not exactly the most romantic way to part, but he knew with all the metal he had on, he'd never make it through without a full-body cavity search. As I walked down the boarding tunnel dragging my carry-on, I was trying to be all Zen about everything. That didn't even last until the end of the ramp.

I wound up with an aisle seat, perfect for tripping rambunctious kids or having my foot continually run over by the refreshment cart. Any guesses what number row I asked for at check-in? If you don't know by now, thanks for not paying attention.

Row eight, of course. My consistency knows no bounds.

Following Finch's suggestion, I stopped a passing flight attendant. "Excuse me, when can we start drinking?"

"Just as soon as we hit cruising altitude," said the attendant.

"Great, can't wait."

While I eagerly looked forward to the liquor flowing, I sat there trying to put the pieces together of how I got here. This was nothing I could ever really explain to anyone; well, at least not in its entirety. And that was okay. There's way too much oversharing to begin with. Sometimes our lives are meant to be just that. *Our* lives. I could just imagine me doing some motivational seminar one day, standing in front of a room filled with aspiring artists, recounting my glorious career. "Uh, hi...my advice to you is...just paint. Can I have my check now?"

Whoever said people don't make sense probably had someone like me in mind. I'd pretty much given up everything to travel 4000 miles alone, to a place where I didn't speak the language, didn't know a soul, and had no idea what awaited me when I eventually returned. But you know what? I'd never been more excited in my fucking life.

Such as it is.

Acknowledgments

Nothing is created in a vacuum, so I would like to thank my family and friends who encouraged me during the writing of this book. Special shoutouts to Brooks Becker, Forman Lauren, and Vanessa Mendozzi for making me look good, and to the systemic support of Bill Kulp, Doug Endicott, Jeff Gelb, Mike Doban, and Simone Sheffield. *Go raibh maith agat.*

CPSIA information can be obtained
at www.ICGtesting.com
Printed in the USA
LVHW052357291020
669934LV00005B/220